HAS THE GANGA STOPPED FLOWING?

HAS THE GANGA STOPPED FLOWING?

LOVE, LONGING AND LIBERATION

SUDHAMAHI REGUNATHAN

KONARK

Konark Publishers Pvt. Ltd
206, First Floor
Peacock Lane, Shahpur Jat
New Delhi - 110 049
+91-11-4105 5065
india@konarkpublishers.com, us@konarkpublishers.com
www.konarkpublishers.com

ISBN: 978-81-993018-4-9

Edited by Dipali Singh
Cover design by Sourish Mitra
Typeset by Saanvi Graphics, Noida
Printed and bound in India by Manipal Technologies Limited, Manipal

Loko bhinna ruchihi…,
(The world is made of people with different tastes).

—*Raghuvamsa* by Kalidasa

Contents

INTRODUCTION

With a Cup of Tea...and Maybe a Slice of Lemon Cake

Through the darkness and fog, I could not see the face of the person knocking at my car window. I was on my way back from Ladnun in Rajasthan to Delhi. The driver had stopped en route for a break. Dawn was still breaking and the coming winter had spread its chill and foggy romance over the night. At that time, I heard this knock.

I rolled down the window of my Ambassador and found a very tall young man. Adonis you could call him, he was so handsome. Wearing the traditional Rajasthani headgear, *dhoti* and *angarkha*, he also wore earrings that glittered through the unsure light. His kohl-lined eyes and a flourishing upturned moustache made him look only more picturesque,

"Do you have some water?" he asked. "My throat is parched. I have been walking continuously."

I was surprised that a man should feel so thirsty in winter, but I had a bottle of water and gave it to him. "*Khoon karke aaya hoon na*…(I am coming after committing a murder you see)," he said casually.

I froze. The fog which was walking into my car through the open window, now filled my head, hearing and senses. Did I hear right?

Yes, I had. "I have just killed the only son, the head of a family," he said. After downing the whole bottle of water, he continued animatedly, "You see the chieftain of the neighbouring village had killed my elder brother, so it was my duty to take revenge."

Therefore, it is, that armed with a rifle, he had gone to the village and shot the chieftain with whom and whose family, they had shared a very long-time enmity. That chieftain had killed Adonis's elder brother, 12 years ago and the elder brothers' wife, now his wife, had kept the memory alive. As soon as her young husband was strong enough, she sent him to take revenge. Not more than 25 or 27 years of age, Adonis (he would not tell me his name), returned my bottle and said, "His son will come after me, but I had to do my duty."

Then he walked hurriedly into the mist, thanking me once again with a salute. As he disappeared into the haze, I caught a glimpse of the wooden handle of a rifle bobbing from under his shawl near his hip.

For many days thereafter I could not forget this meeting … and that I wished him to live. For strangely, I saw a goodness, a vulnerability in a murderer.

I met most of my stories in this manner, sometimes the drama was in my mind. The bewilderment of coming in contact with people or ideas so different from what I could imagine often bowled me over. The desire to share some of the various vignettes of human life came with a sense of urgency and excitement. Scribbled on the back of envelopes and napkins from restaurants, they eventually found their way to my computer.

I realised that every being on this planet has a story to tell. Most of our engagement with life seems to be built in the field of relationships. Attraction and exploitation, loss and learning, are all part of it. The other inscrutable intrigue is death, how to cope with it, what it is and what lies thereafter. Not all our understanding is logical and, therefore, lends itself to some comical moments too. And not all our understanding falls within our imagination and so we discover the truth in "*Loko bhinna ruchihi*".

Princess Indumati was holding a garland in her hand. It was her *swayamvara* and many aspiring suitors had gathered in the palace. One was a brave king, the other a handsome prince, yet another a muscular strong *raja* (ruler) and so on... Sunanda, Indumati's maid in attendance, introduced each aspirant in glorious terms but if Indumati was not taken up by them, it was not a reflection of their greatness (or the lack of it) nor was it Indumati's fault. *Loko bhinna ruchihi*, observed the Sanskrit poet Kalidasa, the master storyteller, in his work *Raghuvamsa*. The world is made of people with different tastes.

It is with the nervousness of sending a loved one out into the world to seek her fortunes that I wave goodbye to my characters as they settle into the pages of this book. I think I have packed everything they could require...if they miss anything, I hope your imagination will help take over....

Has the Ganga Stopped Flowing?

Maharajji, the ascetic who had set up the ashram, met me right at the entrance.

"Welcome," he said and greeted me with a warm smile as I bent down to touch his feet. That is the traditional way of showing one's respect to spiritual masters.

"Look," he said, "just as you came in from this gate, that peacock walked in from the other side at the same time. It augurs well for you..."

I felt a sudden lifting of my spirits. Nothing had gone well for me for many days now. How would the entry of a peacock augur well for my family life, my career, my health? But it was too soon to ask Maharajji. (And I still do not know its significance).

Thus began my initiation into life in the ashram. The grounds spread out endlessly, with the lower range of the

Himalayas to one side and the Ganga River, on the other. Parts of the campus were developed, in the sense that there were buildings; but for most else there were cottages far between in the wilderness. This is where people like me come to recoup…maybe find a life, I thought, as I dropped my bags on the floor and sat down heavily in the cane chair in the room. The room was furnished with a single bed, a study table and chair. On the table was a jug of water and a glass. The room had a huge window, which overlooked green wilderness. The sun was streaming in through that window.

There were 10 people living there in addition to me. Many others, hundreds, came visiting the Maharajji every day. There was a common entrance to the ashram and another to our living area. Inside our living area, we could pass days without meeting anyone, except those who resided there. It was one week since I had come and I had started feeling better already.

Maharajji granted me a special audience in the mornings. It was followed by a session of yoga and meditation. Then I would be with Maharajji while he met the visitors. I would hand him the *prasad* (part of the offering made to the deity), which he would give them with his blessings. Many who came seeking his audience, cried in sheer ecstasy at having met him or after pouring out their sorrows, sharing their fears and getting his blessings. By being present there, I derived a lot of strength. Life had been cruel to me…but I found many people were suffering as much or more. Seeking spiritual recourse, I had begun to feel, was a sign of an evolved state of mind.

Later in the mornings, Maharajji would address a gathering of devotees to give the daily sermon. Then for the rest of the day, we were free.

One afternoon when I was sitting in the verandah of my cottage, watching the wild reeds swaying in the wind along the riverbank, Rampyari came by. Rampyari was amongst the first few people I had met here. Though she lived in the adjoining village, she was doing so many chores in the ashram that she was accepted as an insider.

"I know all of them who come here. Maharajji also trusts only me. Rampyari, get the sheets, Rampyari, check who is at the reception, Rampyari, special guests are coming, organise herbal tea—for everything Maharajji calls me," Rampyari said with pride.

"Would you like some tea?" she asked me suddenly.

"But it is not yet time," I replied, for food and drinks were available at fixed times in the ashram.

"My dear child, do you want tea or not?" she asked. There was a caring note in her voice or was I imagining that every person in an ashram was so inclined?

It became our daily routine. After lunch I would see her plodding her way down the muddy riverbank to my cottage with two cups of tea in hand. Later, she began bringing a jugful because she found I liked more than a cup!

"Do continue reading. I am just sunning myself on your verandah," she said, cracking her toes as she squatted on the floor. It was winter and sitting in the sunshine was the greatest luxury. And here where nature was unblemished, the experience became ethereal. We could hear many birds chirping. A cuckoo flew in and sat on a tree in front of us.

"All my learning is from these beings around us. I have never studied," said Rampyari, shrugging her shoulders.

"Oh! You are lucky. I am trying to learn just that," I confessed.

"Yes, that is true. I find that many people have never spent time to understand the world about them. They think just by reading books they will learn to live well," she said. "Look at that cuckoo. She just moved into the crow's nest up that big tree. She is so clever! She does not waste time making her own nest!"

I put down my book and looked at the bird. "How do you know?" I asked her.

"I live here and keep watching these birds. The crow does not fight with the cuckoo; it lets her be and even takes care of the eggs the cuckoo leaves behind at times. At times, it just builds itself another nest…of course, the crow has no ashram it can go running to!" she said laughingly.

It rattled me. Did she know why I was here? I had told no one but Maharajji. Had he told her? My head was in a spin after that. Was I the crow? Was she making fun of me because I had come "running to an ashram?" All that I had tried forgetting came back vividly and kept reinforcing itself all night. My husband and I had been in love and had a great time for the first two years of our marriage. But after I started touring as my job demanded, we found we spent less time together. And when I had suggested opting for a change in my job, he had protested vehemently, saying I was not to spoil my career. Little did I know a cuckoo was sharing my nest and soon, I would be out. The rest is history. Very soon my marriage ended. My rather insensitive parents thought it was as simple as "getting me married again". But I had fundamental questions about love and marriage to find answers to. At 25, I felt I was done with life. My sense of rejection was killing me and I just could not face anything, even work. I took a long duration of leave and had then landed at the ashram.

So what this lady was telling me made me feel uncomfortable. My mother too had suggested weakly that I should ignore what had happened and move on. "Men are like that," she had commented.

The next day, Rampyari asked me, "What did Maharajji say today?" She was usually cleaning and sweeping at that time when Maharajji gave his discourses and so was never able to attend the meetings.

"He said we have to learn from nature. Nature lives to give. The trees give, even to the man who fells their branches. The earth gives generously to all kinds of people... the rivers flow for our benefit...so in learning to give, we will find protection against sorrows and tribulations of the world," I said, giving her the essence of the invigorating talk of the morning. In fact, I had begun to feel that already. The peace found in serving others was good for me. I had started teaching math in the school run by the ashram and found it very gratifying.

"Oh! But did he not tell you that Nature does not give to the one who does not know how to take? If you do not know how to swim, the river will not stop by and teach you. She will swallow you. Did he not tell you that unless you know how to climb a tree, you would have to wait for overripe fruits to fall to partake of them? I can give you any number of examples, but you people are educated… what am I blabbering about?" she said.

"No, no finish what you are saying," I said, surprised by her clarity of thought.

"We have to learn the necessary skill. Nature gives, but you have to learn the skill to take. The swimmer knows how to enjoy the water. The one who climbs knows how to pluck the fruits. It is the same with life. If you learn the skill, the art of living, you live happily. If you don't, you drown…" She picked up the teacups and walked away before I could stop her.

Her visits started disturbing me. What was she trying to tell me? Just then I had decided I would spend my life doing service and she was upsetting my balance. I could not figure out what she meant. Could I not dismiss each conversation as coincidental?What was the skill one needed to live? To learn to be one-up? To learn to fight for your rights? My thoughts wearied me. I hated the prospect of facing the world, which was so shut out in this ashram. Everything here was so peaceful and so protected…I decided Rampyari needed to evolve. She was just using folk wisdom to baffle me and so I went back to reading about the difference between Advaita and Vishishtadvaita in Hindu philosophy. Maharajji had told me that few people were blessed with an intellect like mine and I should read such books for greater clarity on life. He had even said that the Divine has great plans for me. I was not to be dejected because of one small incident.

"Setbacks are nature's instruments to tell you to pause. In that pause you begin to find yourself. All life is about seeking the self…getting in touch with one's self… and unless we have such experiences that shake us up, we do not think of the Divine. You are getting wiser. Experience of suffering always takes you closer to truth for then you begin to understand pain and, in that understanding, lies your appreciation of laughter," Maharajji urged.

I found Maharajji's advice therapeutic. He spoke so logically! Indeed, without understanding tears, what would I know of the value of a smile? I realised what eventful days I had lived…I had always grumbled about something or the other then.

The next day I narrated to Rampyari what Maharajji had expounded. This time she listened, dumbfounded. Delighted at having impressed her, even if they were with the words of Maharajji, I returned to my book, sipping warm tea. Life was becoming beautiful again. We sat in silence for a long time. Rampyari dozed off. She was an unusually tall person, rather slim and must have been about 50 years of age. She wore no ornaments except for a huge nose ring and a black thread around her neck. A big red *bindi* marked her forehead. She was very fair and had many wrinkles that made her look older. Her father, she told me was from the hills, her mother belonged to the plains. "My husband has been working in the ashram as a gardener and so, I too decided to work here. I do not take any payment. This is my service. Can't I do service even when I live outside the ashram?" she asked with a questioning laugh.

"Of course, that is great. But why do you not take any payment?"

"I get three meals here…food in the ashram is free. My husband brings home money for our small needs. I might as well leave my income for people like you. Don't mind…that was a joke!" she said.

But I did mind. I was miffed and sullen for some time. "Did Maharajji tell you to learn from nature even when it comes to suffering?" she asked, as though to entertain me.

"No," I responded in a monosyllable.

"I did not respond to what Maharajji told you because I did not want to upset you. Now I have done it anyway," she said, placing her hands on my knee.

"Okay, say whatever you have to. I have to get on with my reading," I said to rebuff her.

"Did Maharajji tell you that the river cleanses herself with her flow? That the air drops the heavy particles and moves on to keep itself light and in movement? That the animal licks its own wound to heal, not opening it up for public examination?" Then she left, refusing to elaborate.

I did not want her to continue. Maharajji was teaching me, showing me the path, so I did not need her. But still, the whole night I thought of how to lick my wounds. My father also said, "Stand on your feet and fight the world." They belonged to the age when religion and spirituality had not been adequately understood. I had dismissed what my father had said as a lack of understanding. I did not want to open my wounds for "public examination" as Rampyari had said. In fact, except for my close family and friends and now Maharajji, no one knew what I had gone through. I was strong enough and today had resolved to serve the school and the ashram for the rest of my days.

Soon enough, I got addicted to Rampyari's views. Once she had said something about being alone. I told her this was a godsent opportunity for me to discover myself. She had laughed in her usual scornful way, saying, "Animals, like humans, live in herds…. Lone elephants are often called the mad ones. So even solitude has to be partnered with the experience of family and society to be meaningful." I thought she was being distinctly disrespectful. She again refused to comment on the Maharajji's earlier discourse, which was on peaceful co-existence and tolerance.

Instead, she pointed to some birds hopping, pecking and raising their wings, in close physical contact. "Are they fighting or playing?" I wondered.

She shrugged her shoulders. "I don't know. But both have to go together. We want all play and no fight. That is not possible," she announced.

"But it is," I said. "We just have to build our tolerance."

She laughed. "How much tolerance will you build? Now you hate me…I know, you don't like me saying all the things I do. But I feel you are like my child and so, I still say them. How many aspects will you build tolerance against? And tolerance is such a negative word. Either love or reject is what I think."

"But fighting is so unpleasant," I said.

"Sitting here is pleasant? It is an illusion. You are running away…that does not bring satisfaction. Stand up and fight for what you want…that brings happiness," she said.

"But there are so many people here…so many who come…are they all running away?" I asked a little rudely.

I was about to dismiss her as crazy when she asked me, "My child, someone told me the Ganga has stopped flowing. Is that true?"

How stupid could these villagers get, I thought. And I was giving so much weightage to her views! "How can a river stop flowing…you know her waters come from the snowy Himalayan peaks…" and I went on to tell her about the origin of the Ganga. The Ganga represents ancient Indian civilisation…to the people of India. The Ganges, as she is also called, is much more than just a river. She is deified and worshipped. To even think she will stop flowing is foolish…

"People are polluting her so much that I thought she would have stopped by a boulder to cry and turn back…"

That was the last session I had with Rampyari…an afternoon when I wished I had asked her more questions and made her repeat her philosophies. Maharajji had delivered many discourses but without Rampyari's contentious elaboration, nothing fell into place. Rampyari had shaken me.

I had waited for her every day after that but her husband told me she had fever and had gone to her brother's house. I asked about Rampyari at least three times a day. Then I asked Maharajji about Rampyari and he responded, "She will come." With that prophetic statement and a pleasant smile, he stopped any discussion on Rampyari.

The following two days, I cried like I had before coming to the ashram. Just as I had been getting used to Rampyari and trying to make sense of all that she had told me, she was gone. But her last question had been: "Has the Ganga stopped flowing?" That had shaken me. Indeed, had the Ganga stopped flowing? Then why should I? I packed my bags and left.

Ten years later I went back to the ashram. I used to think of Rampyari very often and thought I could check if she was, by some chance, in the ashram. The Maharajji was hospitable and told a visiting dignitary that I had gained strength from this very ashram when life had not treated me well. It was true. I just smiled when he said his guiding hand had shown me the path. Maybe it had. But there was another hand that had hurried me along.

And, when I found Rampyari, I was elated. She was delighted too. I told her of my life in the past 10 years that had been a good experience. Of how people looked at me as a fighter, an achiever, an authority in my field of work, as....

She laid a restraining hand on my knee and said, "What do you think of yourself? What others say does not matter... after all, the sun rises not because people say it is great..."

And I knew I had more horizons to scale.

When Spirits Rise

Brigadier Rajeshwar Singh took one fleeting glance at himself in the mirror before he heard the front door open. His guests were entering and his uniformed orderly was showing them in.

"What a pleasure, what a pleasure!" he guffawed as he welcomed his guests with open arms. He gave the gentleman a bear hug and turned to his wife.

"Tell me your secret. How do you manage to look more and more beautiful every day?"

The lady blushed suitably and mumbled something.

Brigadier Singh continued, "Oh no! I mean it! And this pale blue makes you look 18."

"Eighteen! You are so naughty!" said Mrs Chawla, waving her hand glittering with diamond rings in dismissal. However, she was pleased to receive his compliments.

Naturally, Mrs Singh did not greet Ritu Chawla with the same gusto.

"*Hello*," she said tersely as they moved towards the sofa to sit down. Ritu Chawla looked at Mrs Singh.

She thought, "What is her first name? Something very nondescript...oh, it's Tapasvini."

Ritu could more or less understand why the charming Brigadier Singh was so lavish with his compliments. Tapasvini was like a *tapasvi* or one in penance. Plumpish, with peppered white hair, absolutely no make-up and to top it all, when she spoke she had a convent girl accent and a voice that made one laugh. It made one feel like saying, "Grow up, Tapasvini, grow up."

Yet, Ritu did not mind coming to Tapasvini's house. Not just because Brigadier Singh was a charmer but also because she hated staying alone at home, particularly in the evenings. Her husband was often away on work and she had to spend many nights alone. Thick vegetation outside the house, the crunch of jawans' boots on the gravelled street, a stray cat mewing and sometimes a never-ending silence made her feel scared. And what she did not tell anyone was that for the past fortnight she had been hearing the sound of anklets...where did they come from? No one in Aizawl wore anklets...no one was around when the sounds came. But they came, that was unmistakable...and the thought gave Ritu goose pimples.

Back in Tapasvini's drawing room, which was the envy of every woman in Aizawl, there was an original painting by Anjolie Ela Menon facing the entrance. Below that was a six-seater sofa and alongside that was a square table full of crystals. "Swarovski...and this one my father got when he was posted to Czechoslovakia," explained Tapasvini.

Tapasvini's father had been a diplomat in the Indian government and that is why she had seen most of the world. She never hesitated to show that off.

A decorative glass table stood on a huge Afghani carpet spread in the centre of the room. The side walls had different wall hangings and Tapasvini would especially draw every guest's attention to a painting on the left wall by the Mexican artist Frida Kahlo. The painting was a self-portrait with a monkey peeping from behind the face of the artist. Frida seemed to have been quite pretty, but suddenly it struck Ritu that Tapasvini had the same expression that the artist had in the painting. Only Tapasvini had thick-set features and a stubby nose.

Personally, Ritu found nothing very great about it, but Tapasvini went into great details about Frida's traumatic life and how she escaped through her paintings into the world of surrealism, adding that she was the third wife of Diego Rivera and so on…

"*Arre*, who cares whose wife she was, *yaar*…"thought Ritu, but somehow men found it interesting…

Mrs Swaminathan and her husband walked in just then.

"Tell me," Brigadier Singh began, "Are you related to Hema Malini? No, no, seriously, you look so much like her." He was now addressing Mrs Swaminathan. This fellow is a flirt, thought Ritu, as she heard Mrs Swaminathan's giggle and the Brigadier's guffaws. "Hema Malini is Iyengar, we are Iyers," Mrs Swaminathan was saying.

Soon the drawing room was full of guests, the usual gathering, but perhaps the first time that they were meeting at Brigadier Singh's house. He had been posted to Aizawl with the Border Security Force (BSF) recently. Ritu sat next to Shalini. Ritu's husband was a transporter, while Shalini and her husband were the owners of the only grocery shop in Aizawl. Shalini's husband Narendra Bothra was wearing a transparent white shirt through which a gold chain gleamed. They were Jains. Shalini wore solitaires, on her nose, on her ears and even on her ring. That was the only thing about Shalini that irked Ritu.

Mr Swaminathan and Joydeep Bose belonged to the Indian Administrative Service (IAS) and were suitably aloof and pompous. Their wives also sat with a certain arrogance, though one wondered why. They were neither in power nor were they dressed with a touch of class. But the men in the room paid them attention to keep their husbands happy. Swaminathan was the secretary, finance, and Bose was the secretary, health.

The conversation was moving almost along predictable lines. Mrs Swaminathan spoke of the problems of getting milk and how Chennai was so far away. Ritu spoke as though she was talking of the one of the great wonders of the world, of how the Mizos do not know Hindi at all! Mrs Bothra and Mrs Bose were whispering to each other about something Mrs Bose wanted to exchange from their shop….

Tapasvini went away to see to dinner. Soon a kind of lull was setting in. Ritu wondered if she should ask Shalini if she had ever heard the sounds of anklets since Shalini lived within a kilometre of Ritu's house.

But suddenly, Brigadier Singh, who was then topping up Mr Bose's whisky with soda, said, "I do not know whether to tell you, but…."

The gathering implored him to say what he wanted to. Hesitantly, the tall man spread his arms dramatically and shrugging his shoulders, asked, "Have you people ever seen a ghost?"

"Ghosts?" everyone started talking together, some saying they did not believe it and some saying they had and so on. For a while no one could hear the other. Ritu was intrigued. Then Bothra's voice survived the cacophony and he was heard saying, "My son is my great-grandfather reborn…this I know for certain…my grandmother told me. He has the same mark on his chin as my great-grandfather had. And you know, we Jains believe in rebirth."

Once again, there was a clamour, and more chatter. Women's voices could be heard talking about the differences between ghosts and rebirth and so on. Some fried pakoras were being served amid a sense of expectancy that hung around the room till Man Friday left the room.

Brigadier Singh cleared his throat and said, "I do not know if I should share this with you all, but when I was posted in Ladakh, I had a strange experience."

He sat down and took a deep breath. The ladies were listening to him intently, but Bose was puffing his cigarette as though he was not interested.

"The Commandant had invited me for dinner. I had to go across very deserted roads to get to the Mess. I was living in a remote area with one jawan as my attendant. It was a very cold winter and we had already experienced one snowfall. But as the Commandant had called me, I had to honour the invitation. So, there I was in my jeep, driving it myself and going towards the Mess.

"It was pitch dark and a blanket of dense fog was settling in. There were no street lights anywhere and the terrain was hilly. I was not very comfortable," said the Brigadier, his voice now reduced to a little more than a whisper. Even Bose puffed harder and an eerie silence descended.

In Aizawl, people lived in fear. It was at the time of the insurgency…Laldenga, the leader of the Mizo National Front had just issued a notice for non-Mizos to quit Mizoram. and had given an ultimate date of 2 July 1978. Just two weeks before, an SDM (Subdivisional Magistrate) had been shot down in Serchhip by members of the Mizo National Front. All the parties and meetings of those posted in Aizawl were actually meant to keep their spirits high. Deep inside, everyone was worried. No one had forgotten the killing of two IAS officers and one Indian Police Service (IPS officer) in Guwahati, a few years ago. So life, death, spirits, ghosts and all such shadowy figures seemed more than real….

"In Ladakh, I heard that people are not always in a hurry to bury their dead. They keep the body at home for many days and cremate or bury them whenever the priest gives them the date. That evening. I had visited a family, which was supposed to be among the wealthy families of the area. They had kept the windows open and cold air was blowing in. You would not believe it, but they led me through their dining room to the adjacent room where a beautiful lady dressed in white lay on the floor. This room was particularly cold. I was shocked to be allowed to enter a room where a lady was lying down."

"She is dead," they told me. "She died five days ago…" and went on to explain their custom of consulting their astrologer.

"I am sorry but I heard nothing…the presence of the corpse disturbed me so. After that they served me tea, but I just could not eat or drink anything."

Silence enveloped the drawing room. Even Frida Kahlo seemed to be listening. "Am I scaring you ladies?" asked Brigadier Singh, "I wonder if I should continue…."

Immediately the chatter began again.

"They keep a dead body for so long?" asked Swaminathan.

"Yes," replied Brigadier Singh. "You know it is very cold there so decomposition takes long and further, they have to take into account the time the visitors would need to come over. This girl's fiancé was stationed further north and the family was waiting for him to return. Honestly, she looked like Snow White, so beautiful, so perfect and her cheeks were still pink…."

"Never heard of such a thing!" exclaimed Shalini. And the others agreed.

"After calling on that family I had set out on my journey to meet the Commandant. When I was driving down to the Mess, her face kept coming back to me. When I was about 4 kilometres away from the town, I saw a huge boulder on the road. I got down to check if there was enough space for me to manoeuvre my vehicle through the side. When I got down, and maybe you won't believe me, I saw a lady in white leaning against the boulder. I went closer, wondering what a lady was doing alone in the darkness. And then when she turned to look at me, I recognised her as the same girl I had seen lying dead in that house…."

Everyone gasped. By now, even Bose could not pretend he was not interested. “I must be sounding silly…” said the Brigadier with his head down.

“No, no, please go on…,” urged Shalini.

“That can’t be true, Brigadier. Are you pulling a fast one on us?” said Minoo, Bose’s wife. She was the “modern woman” in their gathering. She was as she called herself, an “Anglo Indian”. She had short hair and she wore clothes like trousers, jeans and long skirts.

“Oh no, Minoo…no, not at all. In fact, that is why I rarely tell anyone about my experience. It has completely changed me, but I don’t describe to anyone lest they make fun of me. I never discuss this this with even Tapas…but it very much happened.”

“Maybe she was not dead after all,” said Mrs Swaminathan.

Brigadier Singh fussed a little about continuing, but the enthusiasm of his listeners made him go on. “Well, I was shocked. I edged backwards. But she swiftly came and pulled my coat. If she hadn’t, I would have fallen off the road and by God, I do not know how deep the valley was. And then she laid her head on my shoulder…really! I did not know what to do. Within a second, she turned and was gone. She was an apparition in white but she vanished. You would not believe it, but even the boulder was gone.”

“Right here,” said Brigadier Singh patting his right shoulder. “She laid her head right here.”

The rest of the evening was spent in discussing why ghosts wore white and whether it had really been a spirit. Brigadier Singh emphasised, “It disturbs me even now.”

Tapasvini was quite curt when she said she did not believe in such things. She and Bose started talking of rationality, irrationality, modernism and post-modernism.

After that dinner, Ritu was never the same again. She could feel and hear ghosts all day and night. She called up her astrologer in Punjab and asked him if ghosts were real. He answered in the affirmative. He told her she was going through "*Sani dasa*" or the period of Saturn so she had to be careful not go out alone or at night. He performed many *puja*s for her. In return, she paid him many thousands of rupees without her husband's knowledge. The astrologer even warned her that the ghost's anklets she was hearing was real. That got Ritu petrified. He sent her a ring made of amethyst to rid her of ghosts and such experiences. After this, Ritu recounted Brigadier Singh's story to everyone she met.

Many years later, when Ritu was visiting her parents in Chandigarh, her husband told her that Brigadier Singh and his wife lived in Chandigarh too. Ritu was very keen to meet them. The Brigadier had retired and was very warm when they called on him. That weekend he invited them to dinner. There were three other couples there. Tapasvini was much the same. Talking slowly and deliberately, she was now writing regularly for *The Tribune*. Frida Kahlo's painting was in the drawing room and there were many other treasures there, all from Tapasvini's trips abroad. Of course, she still spoke of her father's travels....

Ritu wanted to ask Brigadier Singh if he had ever met "her" again. "Who?" asked her husband.

"The ghost," replied Ritu and she found herself telling her husband the whole story, including her calls to her astrologer because her husband had forgotten everything. Of course, she carefully left out details of how much she had paid the astrologer. The astrologer's efforts had worked, so she did not hear the sound of the anklets after she wore the ring.

Brigadier Singh was his usual charming self. He had invited two other couples. Ritu was introduced to them, but since she was so focused on the Brigadier, she did not pay much attention to the others. She also wanted to tell him about the astrologer.

That evening after a couple of drinks, Brigadier Singh leant forward and began, "I do not know whether to tell you..."

Ritu knew it was the story of the ghost. Her heart skipped a beat. She caressed her ring, which she had never taken off since that day. She wanted to hear the story again and yet did not want to.

Brigadier Singh began telling the story.

"I was in Goa and I had a strange experience," he was saying.

"Oh! Not another one!" Ritu thought, with a mixture of envy and fear.

Ritu felt something surreal about the whole narrative. It was like Frida Kalho was engineering their dinner! She waited with bated breath. And after all the perfunctory statements, Brigadier Singh began. Once again Tapasvini had gone to see to dinner. Ritu felt sorry for the man whose wife did not empathise with his life-changing experiences.

"In Goa, I was walking by the Miramar beach. It was late at night. You know that beach is treacherous even though it looks very calm. I was walking barefoot, enjoying the moonlight and the thrashing waves. I must tell you that evening I had been reading the history of Goa. You know the first Portuguese to set foot on those shores was Alfonso de Albuquerque. When I saw some paintings of his period, there were many people in the background and one particular face caught my attention. It seemed a very Indian face, but the person was in Portuguese attire. A very attractive woman, mind you. Maybe 19 or 20 years of age.

"That night while walking along the beach, I bought some fried fish and went close to the waters to eat. Suddenly a huge wave rolled in and before I could react, something soft and fluffy fell on me. I almost fell down. My fish fries were swept off and rising from my lap was a woman in white… she had just the same face as the girl in the painting… and she was in white. Before I could touch her, she was gone, as though within the waves. You would not believe me, but she was right here," he said pointing to his chest. "Her head was here. And she disappeared almost as quickly as she had appeared. That was the first time I had seen a ghost…I don't know if you believe in ghosts, but what else could she be but a ghost? Later, people told me the lady loved Alfonso but he did not reciprocate. Unrequited love makes the dead turn into ghosts, they said. I can tell you that changed my life… even today…."

The usual oohs and aahs followed and a little confused, she heard them all, about ghosts, spirits, the dead rising and so on.

Ritu felt her finger for the ring. But it had slipped off and fallen to the floor with a ping.

Undying Fire

Hari Prasad Tiwari was in one of those moods. A day before he had been to the doctor who had told him that though he was well, he was to be careful because he had already had two heart attacks and major ones at that. Hari Prasad was not worried about his health. In fact, he did not fear death; of that, he was almost sure. He feared what would happen after his death.

He could not talk to any of his colleagues in the office because few would understand. They often made fun of him. You had to be born in Benares, breathe and live in Benares to understand. Hari Prasad knew one man who understood, Yog Narain Sharma. Punditji, as he was popularly called. He lived in Benares and was one of those people without whom Benares would not remain as it was. He knew everybody and knew about everything that moved everybody. If you wanted to eat the famous *kachori-puri-aloo-jalebi* of Benares, Punditji would take you to the most famous shop, Sri Ram Bhandar in Titri bazaar. He would not only introduce each item to you with relish but would get a free plate for himself, of all that you ate and more! Then he would take you along a narrow *gali* (lane) facing Sri Ram Bhandar to get you the delicacy called *nimish*...a sweet made with the froth that comes from churning milk and leaving it out in the night dew.

It is but right that any introduction to Punditji begins with a description of the food he ate and made you eat because he lived to do so. After he ate to his fullest in Titri bazaar he would indulge himself with some *paan*. He would stuff two into his mouth and two more he would keep in his rexin bag which he always carried with him. Then he was at your service for the day.

What did Punditji do for a living? No one had answers to that. He would be at the Kashi Vishwanath temple at one time, he was going to the Sanskrit college the next moment where he said he was next to the principal in authority. He could organise ceremonies for the dead on the banks of the Ganges and he could help you perform all kinds of *puja*s.

Most importantly, he was the last word on cremation rites. And so it was that Hari Prasad got in touch with him when he was 35 years old. And he had been guiding Hari Prasad since then. Today Hari Prasad called Punditji once again.

"*Arre bhaiya, kah diya na ki ghabrao nahin*...(Oh! I have told you not to worry)," Hari Prasad heard Punditji clear his throat and spit out the *paan* he had in his mouth. Now he could hear him more clearly. "Do you take my words so lightly? After all, it is Yog Narain Sharma's word that you have, so remain calm," he reassured Hari Prasad.

Hari Prasad always felt his equilibrium return after hearing Punditji. He leaned back in his chair. The office boy brought in tea and a *kachori* too. The doctor had advised him against fried stuff, but today Hari Prasad just felt like it. As he bit into the *kachori* topped with *channa*, he thought back about the past.

Hari Prasad had lived with his parents in Benares. His father had worked in Clarks Hotel in the finance department. One day when Hari Prasad had been 16 years old, he had accompanied his parents and younger sister to the ghats. His grandmother had died three days ago in Agra and they had brought her ashes to be immersed in the Ganga. His father had been the only child and his grandfather had died many years earlier.

At that time, while his father had been busy with the rituals, he had seen a strange sight. Three corpses were piled one atop the other and there was a man who was setting fire to them after performing the *puja*.

"Why have you piled three corpses together?" someone asked the man

"We do not have money to burn each one separately," the man had replied.

Hari Prasad's father had heard the reply and gave that man the money to afford separate pyres for all three of the dead. "Why do you waste your money sir? This fellow will just use it for marijuana. He will not light separate pyres," shouted a passerby. Hari Prasad's father ignored those remarks and paid the money required.

In Benares, life and death live in close proximity, one feeding the other. So people who came to the ghats, rarely stopped to grieve the dead. Further they believed that only the lucky ones were cremated on the ghats of Benares and that's why some of them even envied the dead.

With the same alacrity as one leaves the barber's shop after a haircut, the family left the ghat after performing all the rites and rituals. Hari Prasad walked back a few steps with them to avoid the smoke of burning bodies and after telling his mother he would be back in half an hour's time, sat on the steps, also leading to the Ganga. As the sun was going down for the day, the whole river was enveloped in a kind of ochre combined with a strange grey that spread itself thin over the water. Hari Prasad saw the many temples on the banks, all with priests preparing for the evening *aarti*. So many lamps, so many voices all chanting, singing praises of the Ganga made a wonderful sight.

As he was looking around with some satisfaction, he chanced to look at the cremation ghat. He found the three corpses were still burning in one single fire. It appeared that the passerby had been right about the man. Indignant, Hari Prasad got up and walked briskly to the crematorium when suddenly he stopped. After a few seconds he hurried home, not stopping anywhere on the way. Hari Prasad never came to sit by the banks of the Ganga again.

He worked hard to get a job in the railways and was soon posted out. Somehow outside Benares, his memories faded. He got married, had children and ran after the usual promotion and travelling allowances so as to make that extra *paisa*.

When Hari Prasad turned 35, his father died. He was back in Benaras to perform his father's last rites. His father had wished to be cremated at the Manikarnika Ghat, taking fire from Dom Raja, also called the gatekeeper of the dead, a role handed down through generations to provide the cremation fire. All the 19 years that Hari Prasad had worked to erase his last memory of the ghats, went to waste. Every memory came back with a vengeance, fresh as ever.

"Pure Brahmin, do you want fire for your father's pyre?" asked Dom Raja. He sat on a diwan leaning on bolsters at the back and to his side. His mouth was full of *paan* that he was chewing, so Hari Prasad did not understand what he was saying. "*Arre*, who said Brahmins are educated? You can't follow one single word? Have you come here for a picnic? Or are you going to perform the duties of a son on the banks of the Ganga?"

Hari Prasad winced at every word. But the whole process had to be gone through. Dom Raja was asking for 10 *tola*s (units of weight) of gold, Rs 10,000 in cash and 10 bags of wheat as his fee. Hari Prasad could not afford so much. He appealed to the Dom Raja, who continued to insult him by saying things like, "Get yourself a new father or throw him away," "Let the Aghoris take him. He can smear cremation ashes on his skin and live in cemeteries like them."

If Hari Prasad could have cried out loud, he would have. He braced himself to face the unpleasant truth that he had to pay Dom Raja though he could ill afford it. It was at this point, when he was most vulnerable and weak, that he had met Punditji. To help him, Punditji had negotiated with Dom Raja and finally settled for a price of two *tola*s of gold, the rest of the dues being the same.

Then Dom Raja leaned across and from the fire burning in a huge *kund* (reservoir) nearby and handed over burning coal to Hari Prasad. With that, Hari Prasad ensured his father went straight to heaven.

It was and is a belief in Benares that only the fire that is got from Dom Raja should be used for any cremation because this fire had been burning continuously for ages. Lord Vishnu himself is said to have given the fire to the Dom Rajas.

Hari Prasad's grandmother had told him the story about this particular fire. A king called Harishchandra lived in Ayodhya near the banks of the Ganga. In King Indra's court, a question had been asked: is there is a man who, being a family man and leading a normal life, has still remained virtuous and honest? The answer had been: indeed there was such a man and he was King Harishchandra. To test this statement, sage Vishwamitra had come down to earth.

Vishvamitra suggested to the King Harishchandra that since it was his duty to gift, would he also give something to the poor sage? The king agreed readily. "Think," cautioned Vishvamitra so that he would not go on record as not giving Harishchandra a chance. The trusting king did not have second thoughts.

Vishvamitra asked for all the possessions the king had—the kingdom, the oceans and the land around. The king readily gave away everything. The crafty sage added, "No gift is complete without some cash." The king called for 1,000 gold coins from his treasury only to see Vishvamitra raising his hand. "You have given me everything...the treasury is no longer yours. This city of Ayodhya is also not for you to stay in any longer. Even the clothes you are wearing are mine." So Harishchandra had to earn a 1,000 gold coins and pay them to Vishvamitra to complete his gift to the sage.

In order to pay his debt of cash, Harishchandra worked under a Dom, which is the caste of people who burn funeral pyres. His dedication to his duty as a Dom, impressed the gods and he finally passed the test and even got back his kingdom. The Doms call themselves Rajas because a Raja had worked for them. Even today, most people, including Hari Prasad, believe that to get fire for the pyre from Dom Raja was the single act that lent meaning to his entire life.

Hari Prasad went home reluctantly that night. He would have liked to stay there through the night to watch over the pyre. But as darkness descended to embrace the Ganga, Hari Prasad did not have enough courage…it was his old fear that kept him there and it was the same fear that drove him home.

In two years' time, his mother died. Hari Prasad borrowed from his gratuity to pay for her funeral. This time Punditji helped him settle for the same amount in spite of the inflation and rising prices.

Interestingly, Hari Prasad was transferred to Benaras two years before he retired. He came back to live in his ancestral home.

Today Hari Prasad is all of 65 years. He had got his daughter married and spent on her wedding handsomely. His son had also got into the railways. His wife was a happy and contented woman enjoying her grandchildren. Life seemed almost normal till one day Hari Prasad suffered a heart attack. A major heart attack. Everyone thought he would not survive.

But he did and secretly he knew why his spirit did not let him die. He did not have enough money for his own funeral!

Once again all his fears rushed back. He had to provide for his wife's and his funeral. His daughter's marriage had robbed him of most of his savings. And then he had refurbished his house. Even though he took up a job, after retirement, he still would have to save and negotiate with Dom Raja so that he provided enough for his funeral. His son would or would not spend so much on the dead body of his father.

That is why he had got in touch with Punditji again and again. Punditji had assured him the same rates would apply. "But they should not compromise on quantity of wood required," repeated Hari Prasad, maybe for the umpteenth time.

Punditji inserting *paan*s, into his mouth...just grunted.

At the ghat, Suresh, the Dom Raja, did not know if it was day or night. Last night 118 bodies had come in—all of them belonged to rich families so it had been quite a good harvest. Only one family remained in Suresh's mind...that father and his young daughter who was crying inconsolably. The mother who had died seemed to have been very young, maybe forty? And the young girl, surely she was not more than eighteen or nineteen. He had wanted to tell her to be strong. "Look at me," he wanted to say, "I live by cremating bodies...how could I have survived if I was as emotional as you are being now?" But she never even looked at him and when she did it was with the same fear that you would have when looking at Yama, the god of death himself.

"Oh no I am also just like you," Suresh wanted to say and yet he knew the difference. He had grown up with death. Today he had come to celebrate it. The more people died, the more he earned…he did not think so in a bad way. He was convinced that death was the only certainty in life. Every day so many died. He gave fire to more than 150 cremations every day. This was his career—and every career has its opportunity costs.

The opportunity costs had been higher at the time of his father and grandfather and maybe even more for their ancestors. Suresh and his brothers had not much to complain about. His grandfather and great-grandfather had been drunkards. They would hit the bottle early in the morning… well, it is not right to say so because where was no night for them. They functioned all day and night and were so depressed that if they did not drink, they would have died even sooner. Suresh always got angry when he thought of his grandfather and his plight. He used to wear a bell around his neck because no one was to touch him even by mistake. The bell told people a Chandal, an untouchable, was coming and alerted them to keep their distance. His grandfather had also been apologetic about being a Chandal. He felt he deserved only liquor and filth.

But Suresh and his brothers thought otherwise. They were conserving a very important aspect of the Hindu tradition by keeping the fire given by Lord Vishnu, alive. Society owed them something. Rich orthodox Brahmins, who would turn away if they crossed their path, would beg them for fire when a death happened in their family. This showed that they were important to the Brahmins' process of attaining salvation. They had therefore institutionalised their vocation.

"Do not bargain with me," was Suresh's stock phrase. "My rates are fixed."He could see anger and resentment simmer in the eyes of the bereaved standing before him. But there was a similar anger and resentment in his ancestors' eyes...nobody seemed to have noticed them. Suresh ignored the expression of the rich Brahmins. Of course, when really poor people came for fire, he gave away some wood free. They all knew it was not enough, but each one also knew they had done their best...and without discussing the matter further, the relatives would light the fire and go away. Next day, they collected the ashes from the deputy Dom Raja who collected whatever was available. The Dom Raja charged the common man just Rs 150 for it all, wood and fire.

They were seven of them who were brothers. Each day. one brother looked after the ghat. All that he earned that day was his. He, in turn, had deputies who supplied wood, fuel and everything else required for the cremation. These deputies even got customers straight from the railway station, bus stand and other places, where people arrived with the bodies of their near and dear ones. The rates they were paid was fixed. There were also those Aghoris who paid a commission. Aghoris were those people who were involved in tantric practices.

Very few jobs, Suresh thought, could mean just one day of work and six days of rest. And with that one day they earned enough to make them rich. As Suresh stood by thinking, he saw Punditji walking towards the ghat, spitting blood red *paan* on the way.

"*Arre* Punditji, what brings you here? I hope you will never need our services..." called Suresh.

Punditji smiled but did not reply. He had stopped outside the cremation area and called out from there "That Tiwari fellow has had two heart attacks...he wants your charges to be fixed..."

"I have told you, Punditji...why is that fellow so scared?" he laughed.

Punditji laughed too and turned back quickly, spitting once again and calling out, "Take care to supply enough wood."

Suresh knew what Punditji must have seen to turn back so sharply. Just what Hari Prasad saw many years ago. He let such things happen as long as no relatives of the dead were around.

Life is lived at many levels. And one cannot pass judgements without knowing everything about the other level. When humans consume animal flesh, how is human flesh different? Casting a glance and nodding as though to acknowledge their presence, Suresh walked back to his seat amidst several bolsters and cushions and alongside the fire they had inherited.

Outside, on the ghat, some Aghoris were drawing half-burnt bodies from the pyre in the blackness of the night, separating the skull and the flesh...that was their *dharma*, their way of life.

The Village Hero

He was generally referred to as a village hero or Spao. In his *yul* or village, no one called him Tashi anymore, they only called him "Spao". In fact, he was known throughout Ladakh as a hero. Everyone thought of him as a hero, some called him one. And if you saw him you would not believe it. He was a man of medium height, with a balding head (at the time of writing this he was about 75 years old). That which you would call his face was actually a collection of wrinkles which changed shape when he smiled and went berserk when he laughed. His mouth had few teeth and those that were, were not in good shape. His eyes had a smile that could rob any heart. Perhaps that is why he was called a Spao.

He could not hurt a fly. So he did not acquire his status of a hero by killing any villain or any animal. What did he do? Tashi, our hero, was the last of three sons and two daughters. The eldest son seemed to have been a man of authority. He not only safeguarded his parents' land, but added to it. He was the one who had decided that his immediately younger brother should study while Tashi, the youngest. should look after their land.

The eldest brother married a fine lady, tall and slim and known as a beauty in the region. She had two sisters, who were much younger than her and all the eligible men had their eyes on them. The parents of the three girls favoured Tashi. They did not want the second brother because they were not sure he would stay in Ladakh after he finished his education. They wanted their daughters to stay near them. Their first son-in-law proved to be more than an asset. So they spoke with him about getting their second daughter married to Tashi and when they got an agreeable response, they sent over the customary barrels of their locally brewed liquor called *chang.*

Tashi was overjoyed. He had hardly expected such good luck. Diskit was at least three years older than him. But who cared? It was not uncommon in Ladakh to marry an older girl. Diskit was even prettier than her elder sister and she was a little more filled out. When his brother took him to her house as the prospective groom, she whispered to him, asking him to refuse to marry her. He was shocked. Why would he do that? Was he out of his mind? He decided she must be in love with someone else, but Tashi also decided that he would charm her into loving him. He did not refuse, nor did he discuss the matter with Diskit. He married her.

But that is not why he was called a Spao.

Diskit was a shy bride. The wedding was in the month of April. The snow everywhere was just beginning to melt.

Tashi was beaming and joyful and as he led Diskit to their apartment when his eldest brother came to him, looking serious.

"A pack of wild dogs attacked our calf. She is bleeding and in great pain," he said.

Tashi cried on hearing this. He loved the calf, which was just about two months old. "Don't worry," said his brother and told him about the others who were taking care of the calf. But Tashi was too disturbed. He knew that only he could take care of his calf for she responded to him and no one else. He did not take long to decide… soon he was galloping towards home, which was a half a day's journey. He thought Diskit would look sad or upset to see him go, but he felt she looked happy. Maybe her lover was lurking somewhere… Tashi pushed the thought away from his head and thought only of his calf.

He reached home and tended to the calf day and night. After four days, the calf gave up. Tashi was deeply upset. He should have made better arrangements before he left, he thought. He had been so besotted by Diskit that he had forgotten everything else. The thought of Diskit made him straighten up. He should go back to her. He bathed, wore his bridal coat again and took some dried yak meat as a gift for the family. Then, he set off on his horse again.

His in-laws received him happily. All the guests had left. He waited to meet Diskit, but finally, he was told that she was feverish. As a husband he felt he should be near his wife when she was unwell. He went to her room and saw she was huddled in bed, but not lying down. She had a rosary in her hand, her eyes closed as she leant against a pillow with a quilt covering her till her neck—she seemed to be chanting a prayer. They called her and told her that her husband had come. She opened her eyes. What a beauty she was! Black eyes, pink cheeks and red lips, raven black hair and the sweetest of smiles that can be imagined. Tashi wished he could hold her in his arms but instead asked politely, "How are you?'

"I have fever," she replied.

Her younger sister came into the room and touched Diskit."Oh! She is burning hot," she exclaimed and ran to tell her mother. Soon Tashi was ushered out. A doctor was called, but a Lama came instead. He administered some medicine and said she should rest. Night fell and Tashi slept in a room far away from his bride. He was very tired and heartbroken. He fell asleep almost immediately. The day dawned but brought no better news. The fever was unabated. The village medicine man came. He did some prayers…while Tashi was left to his own defences. By evening, it was clear she would take some time to recover.

Meanwhile Tashi's eldest brother sent him a message telling him to return home. "Diskit will come home when she is better," he was told.

So Tashi went once again, galloping across the hills to his village hoping his bride would come soon. A week passed. Then there was unexpected snowfall. So he was told it was snowing and since she had just recovered she should not be exposed to the cold. A fortnight went past. The cold did not abate. Finally, 25 days later, Tashi was all ready to receive his bride in his homestead. She looked gorgeous. Tashi's heart raced. His whole village had come to see his bride. She smiled at everyone, conducted herself with a strange calm and composure. So many people came to him and said he was very lucky. Tashi felt as he would if he was watching the pole star…his eyes were just as dreamy and full of suspense… the distance between them was comparable, he felt. But that was not why he was called a Spao.

The following days were busy and full of activity. His brother had also invited many elders of the village to meet his in-laws. There was festivity everywhere. Another major event was that one of the most respected and revered Lamas of the area was visiting them. The preparations for his visit involved even painting the house afresh. Tashi suddenly realised it was Diskit who was calling the shots. Softly but gently, she was telling everyone what to do. And more surprisingly, even the elders went to her and asked her how the candles should be arranged, what the Lama would eat and so on.

Tashi felt all eyes on him as he walked around his village. He wondered, "Are they laughing at me? A man who is unable to charm his wife…?"

But, their eyes spoke of a different experience…how does it feel to be married to the most beautiful and graceful woman? And pious too. Finally, when someone explained their expressions, Tashi started pretending he could not word his joy, his luck….

The Lama was a kind and wise person. Tashi recognised him at once…he was the same Lama who had visited their house when Diskit had been unwell. He was close to 80 years old. He spoke softly when he spoke and always had a rosary in his hand. His calmness seemed to put people at ease. Everyone except Tashi. Tashi hated to admit it, but he did not like him. Was he jealous of the affection he got from Diskit?

Within a few days of the Lama's arrival, he suggested they visit the neighbouring villages. Tashi found the idea unpalatable. Why on earth would he do that? "Let me live my life my way," he wanted to scream. But Diskit was more than enthusiastic and his mother was also excited. Tashi watched helplessly. Now Diskit looked at him with her lucid eyes, urging him to prepare the donkeys to carry their luggage and horses they could ride on.

Tashi was depressed and that is why every now and then Tashi went for a walk in his village because he liked people looking at him with awe and how some close friends asked him, "Hey, how is it going?" and Tashi would smile…a smile that he hoped would say, "It could not have been better. Poor you…you are not as lucky as I am." But, that is not why he was called a Spao.

Tashi travelled with the Lama's entourage for four days. They travelled all morning and camped by noon. Thereafter they spent time talking to villagers. Diskit and his mother spoke to the women separately. They took medicines, food and clothes to give away and spoke of compassion and love. Tashi was the onlooker who felt he had received neither of the two, except for occasional bewitching smiles from Diskit. What made matters worse was his mother's complete involvement with social work…the only person who could think of him, was also thus practically absent.

After four days, Tashi knew this was how it was going to be. His mother and wife shared a tent, while he slept with the Lama! The Lama, with all due respect, woke up at three in the morning and started chanting. Instead of feeling blessed, as his mother said he should feel, Tashi felt deep anger. Even his dreams could not be completed because he could not lie down when the Lama was up. He was forced to sit under the benevolent smile of the Lama. He even pretended to meditate. The only redeeming feature was that his friends at home thought he was having a joyous time with his wife in the open air. He built new stories to tell them.

On the fifth day, he left for home since his livestock and farmland needed him. The apricots were waiting to be dried, the apples to be boxed. He could not spend so many days away from his work.

A month later, the travellers came home, looking tired yet fulfilled. Tashi was angry with Diskit. He had worked all day in the fields and thought Diskit would notice his absence from home. Perhaps she did. Perhaps she did not. On the third day, when he came back late from the tending the horses and the cows, he could not find Diskit at home.

"Where is she?" he asked his mother.

"Oh, she asked me if she could go and see a friend of hers…she is just 20 kilometres away. Since you have lots of work, she said she would stay the night there and return tomorrow."

"But she never told me," spluttered Tashi.

"I told her I would tell you," said his mother.

Tashi was just about to tell his mother that his marriage needed more attention when his eldest brother walked in.

Slapping Tashi on his back, he said, "Young man, you have spent enough time with your wife. I heard you have not registered to sell our produce at the market in Leh. We are late. Tomorrow the traders are meeting, so you should leave early…meet them, then come back to take the stuff."

He went on talking in this manner. Tashi's head reeled. Though he had not spent any time with his wife, he had missed out on important tasks such as these. He had to package his dried apricots, box the fresh apples…oh! He had so much to do.

Between work, land and livestock, Tashi was completely preoccupied for the next few days. His anger against Diskit smouldered in one corner. And then the worst happened. His eldest brother passed away. That was a big blow to their family. Everything was always done in accordance with his instructions. Everything worked under his benevolent guidance. Now without him they were rudderless. Tashi felt miserable. Instead of mourning with him, Diskit was in her parent's place, consoling her sister.

One day, Tashi woke up to find it had been a year since he had got married. He could not remember any moment of joy. He mounted his horse and decided that he would physically drag Diskit home on that day. He galloped at great speed and recklessly all the way. As he neared her parents' home, he managed to catch a glimpse of her skirt disappearing behind the small bushes. Someone was running away downhill, skipping over boulders…it looked like Diskit…was she running away on seeing him? He jumped off his horse and ran behind her. He grabbed her by her waist and turned her around passionately. Then he stopped. It was Chuskit… Diskit's sister…the one he had never looked at. He found she was beautiful. Was she more beautiful than Diskit? "Not really," thought Tashi. She was mischievous and that twinkle in her eye made her look lively. Diskit's eyes were compassionate ones.

Before he could realise what was happening, she had escaped his hold and had run downhill again. She went down to the rivulet calling, "That was the wrong number! Wish you better luck next time." Her laugh teased him. He chuckled too.

He had a spring in his gait now. He felt light. He galloped into Diskit's house. His enthusiasm was short-lived…for Diskit was not home. She was on one of her social work visits to a village. Tashi was determined to bring her back. He found out the name of the village and went there. She had moved on. He too followed, till he finally found a group of nuns and Diskit with them. Diskit was surprised to see him. He called her aside and said, "Enough of this. Come, let us go home."

Diskit touched his shirt sleeve. "Remember I told you to refuse to marry me? I can't live with you or anyone else, for that matter. I want to become a nun. I need your permission to be initiated," she said quietly.

Tashi did not know what hit him. He had imagined killing her paramour…but now his competitor was the Buddha himself! In helpless rage and disappointment, he said, "I will not give you permission. Do what you wish," and he left that place.

Putting his face down on his horse's mane, he cried as his horse trotted slowly along the route. Tashi could not tell how much time it was, maybe half a day…he probably cried himself to sleep on his horse…he did not want to go back home or anywhere for that matter. People would laugh at him. He would now never get married. In Ladakh, the ratio of men to women was much lower, so generally one woman had many husbands. He had been lucky, everyone said, to find such a beautiful wife…now…will he have to take his elder brother's wife? He did not want to. He wanted to have fun…not be a young husband bullied around by women.

The horse was going towards Diskit's parents' house. Tashi pulled him away. "Now that house is not ours anymore," he told his horse. But, the horse fought himself free of Tashi's hold. It seemed like he was disagreeing with him. Suddenly Tashi picked up a gallop and went back to Diskit's village. This time he was going to meet Chuskit. She was right there, on the way to her house as she plucked apricots. He picked her up and made her sit on his horse, going even faster before she could protest. He went straight to his eldest sister-in-law and said, "Diskit does not want to be with me. Get me married to Chuskit right away."

His sister-in-law loved him as her son and she did as he said for Chuskit also agreed.

Now life turned 360 degrees for Tashi. Chuskit was, of course, madly in love with her husband. They farmed together, they cooked together, they ate together, they lived together. Interestingly, Diskit also came to live with them. Diskit could not be initiated since her husband had not given her permission. The group of nuns had gone back to their monastery, which was quite a distance away. She came to ask him for permission once again, now that he was happily married. Till then she worked in the villages near his house, like she had begun earlier.

Diskit worked very hard, very intensely for the villagers, but Chuskit supported her husband ably in every way. Chuskit gave him three sons and two daughters and helped him in the farm. Diskit helped them too, physically, emotionally and spiritually. She was also very good at writing manuscripts and burnt the midnight oil as she did this. Her health remained indifferent, so she could not be initiated into the fold as a nun for this reason. Her life, though, was more austere and giving than that of an ascetic.

The people of the village saw them in wonder. A man with two wives! He must be like the gods indeed, they thought. That is how he came to be called a Spao.

Tashi liked being called a Spao. He let people think whatever they did. Some years later, Diskit contracted tuberculosis and died.

The secret of the Spao remained buried in the hearts of the women he had married.

Wistful Mist

Sometimes when a picture is just a wee bit out of focus, it gives a feel of fantasy, a glow. That is what Shalini Utsav felt the smog covering the Mughal Sarai railway station was doing to the environs. Everything seemed to have a halo around it, even the light. Some half-concealed kiosks on the platform, the tracks leading to nowhere and moving figures without clear faces—the scene before her was delusory and chimeral. It was getting chilly, the weather was changing. Winter was rushing in. Shalini drew her shawl closer and experienced a strange feeling…like delving into oneself and finding something beautiful there. She was content and she knew why. She had met two people, both of strong character. They had energised her.

When the train chugged into the platform, there was the usual commotion. Shalini boarded the train which was more than two hours late. She had come to attend the conference on Leadership in Education organised by the Banaras Hindu

University. The conference had gone through the routine rigours, talks, points, counter-points, resolutions, but in the end, it had all been about collecting their Travel Allowance. After the conference, Shalini had left early for the drive to the Mughal Sarai station could take time if she got stuck in traffic. When she reached there, she found that the train was two hours late. She had found a seat at the Mishtan Bhandar restaurant at the entry to the station and ordered *lassi*, a refreshing drink made of curd.

"Only *lassi*, *behenji*? We have hot *puri*s and *kachori*s— just taste the *malpoora*s, you will never forget Mughal Sarai," the waiter, who easily looked 60 or more, said with a very pleasant smile. Shalini smiled back and thanked him. "No, I eat light when travelling," she replied.

"*Arre*, *behenji*, all those who come here, are passengers… no one has complained because all the products we make are unadulterated and we maintain such cleanliness that before you board the train you will be hungry again. You are travelling alone at night, so you should not go on an empty stomach…."

Shalini hesitated, then ordered one plate of *puri*s, saying, "Okay, if you say so, but tell me, what is your name?"

"Narain, *behenji*."

"Do you belong here?"

"Well, yes and no. I belong everywhere, but originally I am from Rajasthan."

That was the beginning. Narain narrated his entire life story while Shalini listened, spellbound. Finally, it was time to go and saying goodbye, she went into the station to the AC First Class retiring room.

"Please put down your PNR number, madam," said a woman. Shalini looked up from the sofa to find a lively 50-odd year-old lady holding out a register to her.

"I maintain this place," the lady said, encouraged by Shalini's smile.

"Would you know if I wrote the right number or not? Will you be able to read what I have written?" asked Shalini.

"Oh, *Didi*, why do you shame me? I am here by chance. Compassionate reasons. My husband died six years ago and the children were very young, so I am here...." replied the lady whose name was Buddha Debi.

The train was chugging out of the platform. Shalini looked out of the window and waved to Buddha Debi. As the train moved further, she thought she saw Narain entering the station...or was she imagining it? Dismissing it as a trick her mind was playing on her, Shalini spread her sheet and pulling the blanket over herself, lay down to sleep.

The whistle of the departing train was still ringing in the air. The few hawkers who had stayed on well past midnight also packed up their belongings and made their way out of the station. The coolies too disappeared. Behind the parking lot in some blind corners, you could see them resting, drinking or smoking. The platform was now deserted except for two or three people sleeping, using their air bags as pillows. They were waiting for the early morning train which would come in at 5.30, if it was coming on time, that is. This atmosphere of quiet would last maybe another two hours, by which time newspaper vendors would come in and start making different bundles for different trains, not to mention the *chaiwallahs* who would start their activity too. At this time, one man could be seen walking into the platform with a green plastic bag in his hand. He was a tall man with a comfortable paunch that was just the right size, for it could not be ignored and yet did not become his only definition. He was walking leisurely whistling an old Hindi movie song. He wore a *dhoti* in the traditional manner, folded between the legs to form a kind of pyjama and a cream-coloured vest. His vest was tightly spread over his chest which sported two *rudraksh* necklaces. There was also a small saffron mark on his forehead. A young 60-year-old, he was walking towards the AC First Class retiring room on platform number 3 of the Mughal Sarai railway station.

Her eyes had been right. Her mind had played no trick. It was Narain walking in.

Buddha Debi had swept the floor of the AC First Class waiting room. That was her responsibility. Then she poured the tea into glasses from a plastic bag. Today had been unusually busy as the waiting room had been full. A couple from Japan had come in with their local contact and had been constantly rubbing mosquito-repellents on themselves. Then there had been four people who had come to attend the Ganga Festival. Two men who were travelling by the Rajdhani express had also come in and then there was that lady who had spoken to her for very long. Now at two in the night, everyone had left. It was then that Buddha Debi swept the floor. She heard the shuffle of feet outside and Narain came in with his usual packet.

Buddha Debi shut the door and turned the key in the lock. Narain sat down, and stretching himself, exclaimed loudly with a sigh, Hare Ram Hare Ram. He was tired. It had been a long day. Buddha Debi too sat down, pulling the centre table between them. Wearing a white sari with a blue border, the *pallu* of which came over her head and shoulder, Buddha Debi was a tall woman with a strong personality. She had laid out the plates, tea and water. Now opening the package that Narain had brought with him, she took out hot *puri*s and spicy *cholle*. She distributed them between the two plates.

"What is this?" she asked, holding up another packet that was inside.

"Oh, I got some *kachori*s for Chutki's school tomorrow," said Narain.

Buddha Debi's eyes filled up. "You are so caring. How nice of you to think of her. And how do you manage to get such hot *puris* even so late at night?" asked Buddha Debi.

Narain smiled, pleased with himself. He liked praise. In fact, he was quite impressed with himself. He sat up, tearing bits of the *puri*s and dipping them in the *cholle* before eating them. For the hundredth time, he thought of telling Buddha Debi about his life. Women were always impressed with his story, but he had a secret fear of what people would think if he told them everything about himself. So he had left out some crucial pieces of information even to the lady who had come for the conference.

Narain worked in the Prachin Mishtan Bhandar just outside the station. He worked late and had to be in the shop early in the morning. After lunch, which was about two in the afternoon, his boss would let him go until seven in the evening. That was when he went home. At nights, ever since he had met Buddha Debi, he walked into the station and slept in the waiting room. The timings were just right. He finished work at about one-thirty or two in the early morning when the last train had departed. And in the morning by five, he had to be in the shop to receive the milk. Going home took more than an hour and it was also not too safe at night. He felt he paid for her hospitality by getting her food like *puri*s and potatoes or kachoris with vegetables every night. They would eat together and, of course, Buddha Debi got the tea. And then Buddha Debi would sleep on the floor on one side of the sofa and Narain on the other side. Neither of them slept on the sofa as they did not want to misuse government property. Some fools outside thought they slept together and said so. Narain had contempt for such people, "If they knew me they would never talk like this," he thought.

"Who cares what they say?" said Buddha Debi. "We should be clean in our hearts."

Narain smiled at Buddha Debi, the strong lady who was always praised by her superiors as an excellent worker. She enjoyed one luxury she was not entitled to, which was keeping the AC switched on even after the waiting passengers had left. Sleeping in a closed room without any ventilation would be torture, but for the AC, and she believed she was only keeping herself and her spirits alive. And Narain too thanked her every morning for the cool comfort of the night. Ever since he had started sleeping the nights there, he had started feeling more energetic and cheerful during the day.

Even though both of them went to bed, Buddha Debi could not sleep because she had unfolded the story of her life to a lady who had come into the waiting room. The lady had been impressed with Buddha Debi and said, "You are fighting destiny…that is good. Never give up."

Buddha Debi yearned to tell somebody about her past… how many challenges she had overcome, some through fighting, some by just waiting, submitting to destiny…had she won them or had destiny won, she was curious to ask somebody.

Every time she met someone nice and felt like talking, caution reigned. She suppressed her urge to tell her story because she felt the stigma of being rejected in marriage once would come back to plague her again.

Though born to a family from Bihar, Buddha Debi had lived in a small town in Rajasthan where her father had worked as a daily-wage labourer. When Lakshmi, as she had been called then, was of marriageable age, she remembered how her father had been shocked by the amount of dowry people demanded. There was a period of about five years in their life when every evening after work, her father would literally go from house to house, asking each person to let their son marry his daughter. He came back home every night, very tired after visiting one village or other. Eventually, he found a family that was willing because the parents were unhappy with their daughter-in-law who had not borne them any grandchildren. They wanted their son, Rakesh Kumar Aggarwal, to marry again.

Buddha Debi's father, Kishore Chand, came home that evening with the feeling that he had found the best offer for his daughter. Lakshmi had been a little shocked when he said the groom-to-be was already married. It was not an uncommon practice those days, but it upset Lakshmi when she thought of the woman the man was already married to. Her father did not mind that his daughter was to be a second wife. "The girl is young and so has more chances of being able to bear children," she heard him tell her mother. No one asked Lakshmi whether she wanted to be in that situation.

The wedding was arranged with only one condition. Kishore Chand was not allowed to talk to the groom. "Do not talk to the boy and tell him anything. It is our responsibility to get him to the *mandap* for the wedding," promised the parents. Lakshmi knew her father would not protest. He was not in a position to do so because he felt relieved that someone was marrying his daughter. She heard him tell everyone that it was a wonderful alliance he had secured and if his daughter went into this house, she would be happy. If this marriage went off well, he would have done his duty and nothing could give him greater satisfaction, he claimed. Her father made all the arrangements. At nights he would not be able to sleep. He blamed it on the mosquitoes, but Lakshmi knew the truth. The thought that this family could send his daughter home if she did not bear a child, kept coming back to him. "Well," he once said to her mother, "that is her destiny."

As it happened, Lakshmi's destiny was very different. The groom did not turn up for the wedding! When Kishore Chand went to Aggarwal's house and asked them why the *baraat* or wedding procession with the groom had still not left their home, they said they had called off the marriage. This left her father a broken man. Not only had he spent all his savings organising a lavish dinner, this meant people would think there was something wrong with his daughter and she would now never get married. Buddha Debi did not want to recollect of the trauma of the months that followed this episode.

The very thought of those days made Buddha Debi uncomfortable.

"Too many mosquitoes?" asked Narain.

"*Arre* no. Just got disturbed. Do you still want the AC on?" asked Buddha Debi.

"Oh! Switch it off. Maybe it is the cold that is not letting me sleep either," said Narain.

Buddha Debi got up and switched off the AC. The ache in her body seemed to stem from her heart. As she lay down again, she pulled her *pallu* closer to herself.

She would not be able to tell how many months the three of them, her father, mother and she were in abject misery. The change came when her father took two significant steps. One, he converted to Buddhism. It was a neo-convert to Buddhism who had suggested it. "Buddhism will give you a new identity and fellow Buddhists will help you." The conversion did make her father a happier man. It was as though he had earned a fresh lease of life. Of course, the whole family converted with one caveat. If she, Buddha Debi married a Hindu, she could, if her husband so desired, revert to Hinduism if required to.

And again, Kishore Chand went back to Bihar with his family. He did not change his own name but changed his daughter's name to Buddha Debi. This gave him the feeling few would know about their past. His Buddhist friends found him employment in the town of Darbangha in a Marwari's house where he became the night watchman. The opposite house belonged to a rich businessman. In a matter of six months, he found that the watchman of that house had a son who was working in the Mughal Sarai railway hospital as a dresser. The son was 45 years old. Buddha Debi remembered her father coming home early one morning and discussing the proposal, saying, "Our daughter is not too young either. Let's accept the alliance."Buddha Debi got married to Roop Kalyan and came to live in Mughal Sarai.

Roop Kalyan had been married twice before. His first wife had died during childbirth. The child had not survived either. His second wife had been a pretty young thing who had run away with a helper in the anaesthetics department. Roop Kalyan was thus happy with Buddha Debi who was not that good-looking but presentable. So, she put to rest the fear that she too would run away. She was dark, tall and strong. She bore him two children, kept the house well and cooked delicious meals, which made him feel that finally the right thing had happened to him. But when he was about to turn 60, he died. His children were still young and so Buddha Debi needed to work. Buddha Debi got a job on compassionate grounds, employed by the Railways in the First Class waiting room where she came in at eight at night and left by six in the morning.

"My neighbours take care of the children," she had told the lady who had spoken with her that evening. She hoped the children, a 14-year-old boy called Chotu and a girl, Chutki, aged 11 were safe and had gone to bed while she was in the retiring room.

Shalini got up and switched off the fan in the compartment. The rhythm of the train was soothing and made her feel that life was conversing with her, telling her that there is always more than meets the eye.

Narain was thinking of the lady who had visited the shop at night. Whenever the trains were late, as they usually were, Narain had quite a few customers to serve. This lady had somehow showed such interest in him, that like Buddha Debi he too could not sleep because he was thinking of his past. It was like she had set the juke box of the mind playing.

He too came from a small town in Rajasthan. It had been many years since he had left home with his wife, after a quarrel with his parents. It was then that he had started calling himself Narain, in order to sever any association with his father's name. He had forsaken all the property that his father could have given him. Not much—maybe a small house and some jewels. He had been the only child. But what was he to do with wealth? He just wanted to have two meals a day for himself and his wife, Savitri. He chose the name Narain, which is another word used for the Divine, because anyone who called out to him would also get some *punya* or religious merit. It was believed that taking the name of the Lord brings benefit, even if you do so without thinking of Him. The association with the Divine enhanced his self-esteem.

He found employment in Delhi in the Azadpur vegetable market as a labourer and it was there that he had started thinking deeply about life and its meaning and eventually turned to religion. He maintained a temple in the street corner at the Azadpur market. His wife Savitri wholly supported him.

One day he packed his belongings and taking his wife along, went on a pilgrimage. They went from place to place, visiting all the spots which had mythological significance in the Vaishnava tradition, which gave them fulfilment. Occasionally, Savitri would look wistfully at a family passing by, but Narain was quick to distract her. She loved hearing stories and Narain, who had heard a lot of mythological tales in his childhood, would tell her one and they would once again turn their minds from the pains and pleasures of everyday life to the Almighty.

It was good that they had gone on the pilgrimage when they had because while they were returning from Banaras, his wife had suddenly suffered a heart attack and died at the railway hospital at Mughal Sarai. She had been suffering for some time now and it had always been her wish to die before him. Narain thought of her fondly. He missed her every day. Life had made her suffer emotionally but she always said, "My husband, without you, I would have died long ago."

Narain paused for a moment to think only of her, his dear Savitri. He had felt very lonely since.

That is why Narain had decided to stay on. He too would breathe his last in Mughal Sarai.

During their travel, whenever they fell short of money, Narain had worked in a tea shop or restaurant. It was amazing how restaurants were always looking for help and Narain knew he had a way with customers, like the lady who had come in the evening before boarding the Magadh express. She had set out asking for a glass of *lassi*, but by the time she had left she had eaten *kachori*s, *puri aloo, jalebi*s and even *malpura*s.

If Narain worked anywhere even for one day, the owners of the restaurant would beg him to stay on forever. But Narain had to admit that he had looked back anew at his life after speaking to this lady who had come for the conference in Banaras Hindu University. He wanted to talk more and more about it to anyone willing to hear him. He felt he had truly held the spirit of love above all in his life.

Narain slapped a mosquito dead. If Buddha Debi got disturbed…he would tell her. He winced at the thought of his fear. But Buddha Debi was a sensitive woman…she would not call him impotent. But no, Buddha Debi did not stir. Narain turned to his side, wondering if he should wake her up and tell her the story of how he, earlier known as R.K. Aggarwal, had left his home refusing a second marriage his parents had tried to arrange…just because Savitri and he were childless.

Shalini woke up all ready to get down. The train would draw into the Etawah railway station at five in the morning and she was nervous she would miss the stop if she went back to sleep. When she checked her mobile for the time, it turned out to be only three-thirty in the morning. Very restless, she sat back and decided against sleeping. It was pitch dark outside the window…so many places, so many people, connections, coincidences, so much to the world we do not know of, thought Shalini. And every person, perhaps every being had a story to tell….

A Heaven Out of Reach

This morning I felt I was back in Kumbakonam, Bakhtapuri *Agraharam* House Number 96. Bhaktapuri Agraharam was the street in Kumbakonam where Brahmins of the town lived. My father had been posted to Kumbakonam and we had found this house to live in. This sprawling bungalow was rented by my parents for Rs 40 per month, a princely sum in the early 1940s.

I could see Cheemachimama sitting in the *thinnai* (verandah). Cheemachi was his name. Mama means uncle. We children called him Cheemachimama. There were three *thinnais* in that large house. We used to play Four Corners in the second *thinnai* which had pillars. Cheemachimama sat in the first *thinnai*. This was at least 75 years ago.

Cheemachimama belonged to Pundi, my parents' native place, and by that virtue alone he was in the *thinnai* of our house. Perhaps he was also related in some distant way, I do not know.

He was a short man, with hardly any hair on his head but a fairly thick beard. The beard was not long, but it surrounded his chin and mouth like a small white forest. Judging by the colour of his beard, I reflect he must have been above 60 years of age, at least.

He endeared himself to children. He would put my little nephew, about a year old, on his lap and would keep slapping his thighs saying "Rama, Rama," and the child would go to sleep. He used to help my mother too, I do not know how, but I would even see him hovering in the kitchen at times. For most part of the day he would keep guard, sitting outside in the *thinnai*.

The days he had an oil bath, every passerby would know because he would be missing from the *thinnai* for several hours in the morning. He would drip with oil, maybe he poured a litre of oil on himself! The bathroom was rather large. It had a well to one side and firewood burning on the other. A huge copper pot called a *thavale* would be sitting on the fire. Cheemachimama would fill the *thavale* to the brim with water from the well. He would then dish out the hot water with what was called a *shombu* (small jug). He would take a full hour to have his bath. And that is why he always preferred to bathe the last.

Cheemachimama was a hearty eater. He would eat on a banana leaf and a white mountain of rice would be heaped up on his leaf…

There is a story behind why Cheemachimama ate so much. Long ago, when he was but 12 years of age, he got married to a girl called Lakshmi. She was only seven years of age. Even though Cheemachimama's name was Srinivasan, people called him Cheemachi. His mother passed away when he was two years old. His father was an agriculturist, who was out in the fields most of the time. He never remarried. His son grew up as that was the only way of life. He ate when his father came back from the fields and slept at the same time that his father did. For some of the day, he played with the cows in the house. His grandmother, who lived with them, would shout out to him saying, "Go, have a bath. She went leaving her son with me. Is it possible for me to look after that rascal?" Cheemachi hardly heard what she said. He went to bathe after she had called threateningly for the umpteenth time. After that, he went to school.

When he was about 12 years old, his father took sudden interest in him. Also, his grandmother applied oil on him and they even gave him new clothes to wear. He sat next to a girl and they said he was married. Cheemachi knew that boys his age were discussing marriage, but they generally got married only when they were 15 or 16 years of age. Cheemachi wondered how he was selected for this favour at such an early age. And he wondered rightly, for there was a reason. Lakshmi was born when the moon was in the *Ahilya nakshatra.* Ahilya nakshatra is the ninth of the 27 stars or lunar mansions in Indian astrology. It corresponds to the constellation Hydrae. Astrologically that was not an auspicious nakshatra to be born in. The astrologer told the family that this would be a problem for the girl because she would have to get married to a boy whose mother was no more. *Ahilya nakshatram* was bad for the mother-in-law. The only fitting candidate in Pundi was Cheemachi, because his mother was not alive. Lakshmi's parents quickly finalised the marriage although Cheemachi's father had suggested they wait for a few years; Lakshmi's parents would not hear of it. They feared that Cheemachi would get a better alliance elsewhere and their daughter would remain unmarried! No, no, they would not let the match go.

After his marriage, his father sent him to Madras (now called Chennai) where he was put in a hostel. Since the hostel was close to his school, they were lucky to have found it. That was because Ponnuswami, a farmhand at Pundi, had a brother-in-law called Veluswami, who worked as a peon in this hostel. Cheemachi's father was very happy because Veluswami would keep an eye on his son.

Cheemachi began to take his studies seriously. Even during the holidays, his father never brought him back to Pundi. Instead, Veluswami got him part-time jobs at some office or the other. Veluswami's family was nice to Cheemachi. Veluswami had a daughter called Daamala who was to marry Ponnuswami's son. Daamala had been to Pundi several times and knew Lakshmi, so sometimes Daamala and Cheemachi would talk about Lakshmi. She would describe how beautiful she was and Cheemachi would listen. One day, Daamala asked Cheemachi, "Have you seen her of late?"

"No, of course I have not. I have not been home for the past five years," replied Cheemachi.

"Hmm...," said Daamala thoughtfully. Then she confided, "I am very scared to marry Ponnuswami's son..."

"Why?"

"He is very rough and rude...I have seen the way he behaves with the people around him. His language is so crude...you know that is what happens when you do not have any education. He has a vegetable and grocery shop, but he is not nice to his customers…"

"Oh but he will be nice to you," said Cheemachi reassuringly. Daamala had studied up to Class 5 since she had lived in a city and in those days that meant she was highly educated.

"I wish everyone was as kind as you," said Daamala and Cheemachi blushed.

After five years, he returned to Pundi. He had completed his Secondary School Leaving Certificate or SSLC as the school final was called those days. He was a confident boy now, could apply for a job as a clerk in any government office and wore clothes that were almost like an Englishman. There was only one problem. He was just 4 feet 10 inches in height. He did not feel that was a problem because his mother, they told him, was also short. He came back smiling because now Lakshmi had meaning for him. He was delighted in the knowledge that he was married and looked forward to taking her home with him.

Lakshmi's parents were also waiting. Their daughter had just attained puberty and they wanted her to be sent to her "rightful" place. Or else she and Mangalam of the neighbouring house were always playing in the garden with their *thali*s (the symbol of marriage) hanging around their necks. "What would people say?" Lakshmi's mother kept saying, "It is five years since our daughter got married and she has still not gone home. They will think she has not attained puberty though we did invite all the women of the neighbourhood when she did."

Lakshmi was also quite pretty. She had a fair complexion and so everyone said she was like Queen Elizabeth herself. There was one problem though. They also said Lakshmi should have been a boy and joined the police force.

Why they said that you will know when Cheemachi and Lakshmi finally met. She stood towering over him because she was 5 feet 10 inches! Her heart crumbled to see this hopeful aspirant, who called himself her husband, hardly rise up from the ground. He, in turn, felt crushed to see this skyscraper who made him feel small. One or two inches, he could have always managed. The marriage began on this note of disappointment. He could not cuddle her in his arms and she could not look up to him. Their ways did not meet.

Cheemachi's father was also shocked. "What is this?" he said to Lakshmi's parents in a piqued tone, "You know girls should not be fed so much…what have you grown here, a coconut tree?"

His abrasiveness made Lakshmi cringe and her parents apologetic. Cheemachi did not mind. "Let us give it a try," he told his wife that night. "We will not go out together, but otherwise we can be loving."His wife did not reply.

Days drew into months and Cheemachi found a job in the local *tehsildar*'s office (a *tehsildar* is a land revenue official). He also started eating more and more, hoping the food would pile up on his head and add to his height. That is how he developed an enormous appetite. He did exercises that he hoped would make him tall. All that happened was a slow but steady addition to his girth.

Once in a while, he met Daamala, who had also got married by then. Her husband was always lying drunk outside the shop and she was managing everything plus her infinite number of children…they just seemed to keep coming! He never spoke to Daamala because it was not done. They knew what the other was thinking and moved on.

One day Cheemachi's father died. Meanwhile, Lakshmi's father had also passed on. There had been no progress in Cheemachi's marital life, but he remained hopeful. Lakshmi was always busy. She had many friends and attended all the festival celebrations in the temple, so almost every evening she was out. When she came back she locked herself in the small room inside and slept. Cheemachi was left in the lurch. Once his father died, her disdain for him turned into animosity and came out into the open. She called him "Kutte" or Shorty. It sounded so disrespectful. Hardly how wives were expected to address their husbands, mused Cheemachi. She also seemed to be taking revenge on Cheemachi for the people around her calling her "Nettai" which meant tall. They would say, "There goes Nettai…."

Passersby and neighbours would hear them shouting at each other. Actually Cheemachi rarely raised his voice. He thought one day she would love him. After all, he was short and she was justified in being disappointed. But he was also a nice person and loved her. He brought home jasmine flowers, he brought special halwa from the one and only restaurant in the village, but the ice did not melt. Instead she made fun of him. "Oh! the jasmine string is almost as long as you…" she would say and laugh. Cheemachi would try to smile, hiding his hurt soul.

Then she started making him cook, she would abuse him in more ways than one…and finally, she started beating him. Then it became too much for Cheemachi. He could not reach up to her to beat her and people said he used to jump up to reach her face and slap her. Even then he was barely successful.

The next we know is that Cheemachi was visiting his friends and staying with them. That is how he was with us in Kumbakonam. What happened to Lakshmi, we do not know. Cheemachimama never spoke of her.

He stayed for long periods with us. Cheemachimama had some land in Pundi and he would periodically go back to attend to it. When he came back from Pundi, he got us plenty of snacks and gifts. Those days there were not many hotels, or rather the Brahmins never frequented them, so new tastes always brought joy.... But he never took the eatables inside the house. He used to put them in steel tiffin boxes and keep them by his side. My mother would not have them, so he would not even offer any to her. We did not find it unusual because our mother never ate anything from outside due to her orthodox beliefs. He would also bring some earrings or rings...I would love them but my mother would say, "Why do you bring these things, Cheemachi? There is no need you know...." But, Cheemachimama always brought us something. He once gave me a wooden doll and on another visit, a sari! He bought me the sari when he sold most of his lands and, therefore, earned money.

Cheemachimama has never spoken to me seriously about anything, but one day he told me, "Study well. Education refines you."

Cheemachi went to Pundi, even after he sold most of his lands. I do not know why. Of late he had started hiring a taxi to go to Pundi. He had become old and was not able to go by bus or wait for the train and rush through the crowds.

One day he fell ill and could not walk. He needed full attention.

No one thought of his wife. Maybe she was no more. Who would look after him?

Even as the elderly people at home were wondering how to take care of him, one morning a tall, strong and smart-looking lady came to our house. With great care and affection she practically carried him into a taxi and took him to her home. I stood transfixed.

Her name, my mother told me, was Daamala. Oh! I knew who Daamala was! That day, she took him to her house…

We hear that he was taken very good care of by Daamala for quite a few years thereafter.

The Bejewelled Feet

Javara Ram was happy to be a gardener on the university campus. He received a fixed amount every month as his salary, which he did not even bother counting. He worked all seven days of the week...not because he was asked to do so, but he had nothing else to do. He worked because he loved plants and gardening. He was free to do what he pleased. His job kept him occupied.

And then suddenly, his salary became almost threefold and he was informed that his job had been made permanent. He laughed at this. The ways of the administration had always amused him. When they told him not to work on Sundays as they were always holidays, he shrugged his shoulders but not before asking if plants stopped growing on Sundays! Jawara Ram, who had no idea of his age, was by guess in his mid-50s. It was his habit to run his fingers through his grey mop of hair, brushing it back to reveal a very peaceful countenance.

He could not be called handsome, but there was something very fresh and untouched about his face. It was endearing.

Javara Ram was an unassuming man. A resident of Titli, a small village about 20 kilometres from the university, he had grown up in the place and had tilled his father's land. He had not known what a school meant and had never seen one till recently. In fact, he had not stepped out of Titli village, except once to get married. Titli, which was the world to him, was located in a very backward and dry district of Rajasthan, housing barely 40 families. His wife, who hailed from a neighbouring village, had been a shy bride, but perhaps because he had been a bashful young man, she had emerged from her cocoon of hesitancy and inhibitions to almost lead the house. She had been a wonderful daughter-in-law. She had borne him a son and all three of them were happy to eat whatever they were able to produce. She was quite tall for a woman, plump and light-eyed, with a very pleasant smile. If her nose had been a little sharper or her lips a little thicker, she would easily have been the most beautiful woman in the world, thought Javara Ram. She always wore a voluminous flared skirt with floral prints and a long blouse. Over that she threw on her *dupatta* so that she could cover her head and face when necessary.

She had given birth a few times after their son, but none of the babies had survived beyond the age of one or one and a half. One succumbed to jaundice, another to diarrhoea and the other with a high temperature had just died one day. They poured all their love and affection on their one and only son. the one who would take forward their lineage.

In time, Javara Ram's parents died and his son grew into a smart young man. Tall and lean like him, but fair like his mother, he also had her light eyes. He helped his father with cultivating their land till one day he came home to say that he wanted to go to Dubai to make money just as his neighbours did. He had barely studied up to Class V and had just about learnt to write his name. However, no educational qualifications were required for the job he was going for. He was strong, heavily built and could work hard. The family did everything, even sold most of the land to help him go to Dubai. He brought back plenty of money after a year, and renovated their house completely. They could have bought back some of their land, but both Javara Ram and his wife felt they did not have the energy to till land any longer. Their renovated old house gave Javara Ram and his wife great happiness and pride. This was their first *pucca* structure. It had a bedroom, a kitchen and a bathroom. Outside the bedroom was a covered verandah, which is where they sat most of the time. They had built the bedroom in anticipation, waiting for their son to bring home his bride.

With prosperity came marriage and the son got married to a pretty woman, or so the women said. Javara Ram had never seen her face for the women always drew their sari or *dupatta* over the heads as veils before their fathers-in-law. His wife had told him that his daughter-in-law had sharp features, a pleasant smile and was fair-skinned. He could see very clearly that she was tall and had a buxom figure. He could recognise her feet anywhere— bedecked with anklets and rings on her toes, they looked soft. She wore a special anklet that caught Javara Ram's eye...his wife told him that it was a family heirloom that had belonged to their daughter-in-law's grandmother. It had a row of polki diamonds and they glistened without warning. She wore two toe rings on both feet, one pretty large with a green stone on it. The sole of her feet bore the ochre colour of *mehendi* made from the juice of henna. Javara Ram felt his daughter- in-law was a girl of taste from the manner in which she had applied the *mehendi*. The amber-coloured patterns were a beautiful contrast to her fair skin.

Javara Ram and his wife enjoyed their status as in-laws. They would sit discussing their lives on a wooden bench in the verandah. They could say the same things over and over again every day and still find their conversations interesting. When their son was away in Dubai, Javara Ram's wife slept inside with her daughter-in-law. When their son came back, he refused to let his mother sleep out in the verandah and so enclosed part of that small space, just big enough to accommodate one cot. Javara Ram and his wife were proud of their son's concern.

Within a year of his son's marriage, they had a grandson. By the time the second grandson was born, which was three and a half years later, Javara Ram lost his wife. She had died suddenly one night and they never knew why. Some said spirits were hovering about the village, while others said that even God could not stand their happiness. Javara Ram did not complain. He had had a good life and was now also ready to go. When he lost his wife, Javara Ram decided he should keep himself busy. If he was at home, he constrained his daughter-in law's movements. She would not come out of the house …and what would she do if she was confined in the room the whole day? She had to wash clothes, scrub dishes, buy milk and do many other chores. So he tried sitting in someone's fields, but it was too boring.

His son continued to work in Dubai. He came home twice every year for two or three weeks and only wrote or sent money for the rest of the time. His letters informed them about the money he was sending or when he planned on coming. None of them could read so often the postman read out the letter to them. Nowadays he called…he had got his wife a phone. That contraption vastly improved their lives for he and his daughter-in-law never spoke to each other. If there was any message to be conveyed, the grandsons acted as messengers. Usually, the message was to tell him his son had called. So now that his daughter-in-law was talking to his son every other day, he was happy. He felt all her needs would be communicated to him one way or other. But he never talked on that tiny phone as he just did not feel confident enough to do so.

Deepa Ram, his neighbour, was a kind, helpful man, a little younger than Javara Ram. Deepa Ram and his wife did not have children and so were always helping people of the village. Deepa Ram's wife was a good lady except that she gossiped, so if one went to her for help, the whole village would know what the problem was. Javara Ram's wife rarely took domestic matters outside the home and her daughter-in-law seemed to be similarly inclined.

Since Javara Ram did not have much land left and so had very little work to do, he was interested when someone told him to go to the university and ask if there was any job available. It was the only university in their district. Many people from his village had got employment there as sweepers, peons, chowkidars, clerks and so on. He got the job of a gardener almost immediately and was happy. It was a long walk to the campus but Javara Ram decided to try it out.

The university paid him Rs 500. From then on he left home early at six in the morning. He preferred to walk for two hours to get to the university although a bus plied on this route. It made him feel energetic. He walked erect and tied a white cloth as his turban in the typical Rajasthani style when the sun was too sharp.

Just a couple of kilometres before the university stood the Balaji temple. Inside the premises, there were shrines for the divine idols, Shiva and Hanuman. Hanuman, the monkey god, was also called Balaji in Rajasthan, the shrine dedicated to him being the main one. He liked the priest there, a nice young man. The priest was still trying to set up the temple as its owners were in a far away city. One day, after doing the *aarti*, or the religious ceremony. the priest told Javara Ram, "I have a *dhol*, a large drum, but I just need someone to play it. That man should follow rules like celibacy, which is very important."

When the priest heard that Javara Ram's wife had died, he decided Javara Ram was the right candidate. From then on Javara Ram played the *dhol* every morning and evening for the *aarti* with flourish. An attractive man, Javara Ram sported a lithesome body, but was totally unaware of this. He wore ear studs as many Rajasthani men do and had very deepset eyes. He did not have the typical moustache which many Rajasthani men did, but was clean-shaven. When he played the *dhol* he looked as though he was straight out of the movies because of his frenzied movements during the crescendo of the *aarti* and always captivating to watch. Many people were often torn between the desire to watch him or the idol in the sanctum sanctorum. When he played the *dhol*, Javara Ram looked almost ethereal. Women were captivated by him, but he was blissfully unaware of the effect he had on the onlookers.

The priest offered to pay Javara Ram a salary, but of course he refused. "I do not need money," he told him. "I am here for the joy of playing in the temple."

In his routine, Javara Ram wore a white *dhoti* and a grey shirt for work in the university. This shirt had only four buttons and the rest of it was like a kurta that had to be slipped down from the neck as a pullover. This style was typical in Indian villages. He tied *his dhoti* as the typical Rajasthani would, going between his legs to form a kind of pyjama. When he came to the temple, he would change into the *dhoti* along with a vest that was traditionally Rajasthani. That vest was also white but was called an *angrakha* locally, with the chest pieces overlapped. After playing the *dhol*, he would wash his *dhoti* and vest and put them out to dry for the next day.

When he reached home, he would clear his throat and even as he pulled his shirt over his head to take it off, one of his grandsons would bring a steel *thali* (plate) with his dinner on it and a *lotta* (a jar-like glass) of water. He would hang his shirt on the clothesline in the verandah, seat himself on the wooden bench and eat. He never asked for more nor did he ever waste a morsel. After dinner, his daughter-in-law, it would seem, waited for his loud burp, which always came in a succession of three! She would then switch off the light inside her room. His grandsons, aged six and two, would have gone to sleep by then. The front door to their house never opened when he was in the verandah, except when his grandsons came out to give him food or to run out and play. They always carefully closed the door behind them.

On the first day of every month when he was paid, Javara Ram would give the whole packet to his grandson, who would hand it over to his mother. What she spent, what she saved, if that money was enough, Javara Ram never asked.

In winter that year, Javara Ram's son came home as usual. He told his son about the increased money he was getting from the university. "Stop working, Baba," he advised his father. "The boys are getting older. Teach them our way of life."

Of course, neither Javara Ram or his son took that conversation seriously. Then one day when the son was to leave at the end of the week, he developed fever. Swiftly, within three days, his fever grew worse and Javara Ram's one and only son died.

Everything was lost. For a few days Javara Ram grieved intensely. He did not know what to do. But when he saw his grandsons, he knew exactly what he had to do. His work became important.

His son had brought back plenty of savings, but Javara Ram had given up counting money for a long time. His neighbour, Deepa Ram, had told him that the funeral had cost quite a bit. Deepa Ram had done everything...taking control of the cremation and the other ceremonies at home. Deepa Ram's wife had been by his sad daughter-in law's side throughout. She now wore only black and all her jewellery had been removed.

Javara Ram was in a daze, but his mind kept telling him that the two little boys had to be brought up.

Deepa Ram had advised him to talk to the vice chancellor and get his daughter-in-law a job. But Javara Ram had spent one night thinking about it and by morning had decided that he would not do so. In his family, no woman had ever worked, not his grandmother, not his mother, not his wife. His daughter-in-law too would not have to deal with a job. His dear son would be hurt if he knew his wife was working.

Javara Ram did not give up playing the *dhol* at the temple but kept waiting for the priest to make the payment offer again...

In about six months, things had fallen back into routine. Javara Ram left early in the morning and came back for dinner as usual. But now he found his walks to the university wearisome. He did not want to take the bus because he felt he should save that money instead. His grandsons had started going to school. He began taking interest in tips given to him at the university, running errands for the administration. The cycle of life seemed to have gone back to the beginning all too soon.

That night, when Javara Ram came home and had dinner, the light in the bedroom went off as usual. Javara Ram, who had not slept since his son had died, lay staring at the walls, when he heard the door open slightly.

A bare foot shorn of the jewellery he had come to know so well and the *mehendi* he had admired, stepped out and then after a little hesitation, went back in…the door was left open….

Javara Ram sat up…

Cheating Death

The phone rang again. It was the third time that the call was from the same number. Ramesh was the name that appeared on the screen. I was too nervous to answer the phone. When it rang again for the fifth time, I answered.

"She has gone," he said.

"Who?" I asked.

"My wife," he replied between heart-wrenching sobs. I just cried with him.

What to else was there to do?

Ramesh is the son of Govind who has practically grown up with me. When we moved into our own house, my mother was thinking of hiring a house help when this young boy, barely 15 or 16 years old, stood at our doorstep. He told my mother he had seen us coming to the colony when we were in the process of building our house and was currently doing odd jobs at our friend's house in the colony.

His face was bright and he had a warm smile. What made my mother decide to hire him were his words, "I am trying to appear for the 10th Class examination through the Open School. If you let me clean your house, I will also learn from you brothers," he said, looking towards me and my two brothers.

He began by cleaning the house, which he did so well... but soon everything about the house happened because of Govind. The booster pump did not work? Call Govind. The fuse has blown out? Call Govind. There is a snake in the backyard? Call Govind. The shirt has to be ironed and there is no electricity? Call Govind. After two years, Govind even scraped through his 10th Class examination. Now the family's preoccupation was to get him a job.

In the meanwhile, Govind got married. He brought home a pretty bride named Rajeswari. We thought he got a girl he deserved because she worked with him, laughed with him and was really good-looking. Even though no permanent job was forthcoming, Govind did odd jobs and we increased the salary he got from us. However, his family started growing—one son, a second son and a daughter...Suresh, Ramesh and Ranjana. Now the family preoccupation became funding Govind's brood.

Some years later, we managed to get Govind a government job as a cleaner and he started drawing an adequate salary... it meant a steady income and lots of respect from his community. He would soon become permanent in his job and then it would be a life of ease...he told me about the strategy the seniors followed. They would come in in the morning and sign in their attendance and then go back. People like Govind who were temporary would fill in for them, do all their work and more. In the evening, at the office's closing time, the permanent employees would saunter in again and sign for the end of their day. So during the day they actually did other jobs or some just lazed around. Many of the permanent cleaners acted as touts.

They were in the transport department. Those days nothing was computerised. This made it easy for touts, who promised to get the work done and get their share. Govind soon learnt the ropes and we found everyone asking him for help to get their driving licences, special number plates, permits to ply tempos within the city and so on. He put on weight and grew very confident. My mother felt an instinctive misgiving and told him, "Do not take money to get licences and other work done for the seniors."

"Oh no, madam," he said, switching on his charming smile. "Will I ever do that?" My mother believed that he would not.

"And they are all *goondas*, who intimidate others. Do you know there are many gangs there? The area is divided under different gang leaders and they each operate in their area. I help people without their knowledge and they tip me because I do not charge them. They tip out of choice."

Since his work was becoming demanding, he was erratic in coming to our home. His wife Rajeswari was very pleasant and equally smart. She charmed my mother and helped her in the household efficiently.

A few years passed. We, my brothers and I, got married and none of our spouses liked Rajeswari. My brothers and I believed it was because of the liberty she enjoyed with our mother…they were a tad jealous, we laughed. But, they had their own stories to tell. They all felt Rajeswari stole their jewellery and the cash left lying around, but she was never caught in the act. So their dislike remained a murmur.

One day, we received a phone call from somebody asking for Govind. He claimed to be from the transport department. We were surprised. "He has not come for work for more than a month," they told us. But what irked us was that the person who spoke to us did not sound friendly. On probing, we heard him say, "Sir, does Govind work for you? We are filing a police complaint against him…."

They did not file a police complaint, at least to the best of my knowledge. The reason I say that with confidence is because we later found the call was not from the transport department. But Govind was in trouble. Rajeswari confirmed that he had stopped going to work and was drinking heavily. The story that we could put together was that he was helping somebody because of which he was stepping on the toes of one of the gangs operating (as he had already told us). He had received a large "tip". They thus got after him for robbing them of their income. For all the gangs operating there, Govind was becoming too smart.

I feel he had started operating like a gang leader himself. Now the gangs were after him. When I went to the transport department and met the officer there, he had only nice words to say about Govind. But the gang leaders had threatened Govind. He did not dare tell any of us because he felt we would not understand how cruel and wretched they could be. He instead went into hiding and spent his time drinking.

In short, he soon became such a drunkard that nothing helped. We tried everything possible, including Alcoholics Anonymous, but nothing worked. He just started avoiding us.

Rajeswari continued to work for us. Her elder son got the job of a cleaner in a private office. The younger son Ramesh used to work with her, for us and other houses. He was as smart as his father, but a bit of a shirker.

As time went on and our children started growing up, we moved houses, sometimes cities and had different house helps. Soon Rajeswari and Ramesh lost our favour, although they still worked for our mother. Our wives were now indifferent to them for the duo did not work directly for us.

Our mother's obsession now was to get Ramesh a job. We tried to place him in many offices but he was never regular. Finally, we managed to get him a government job too and gave him long hours of advice on how not to fall into a trap like his father did.

Time has an uncanny way of rolling past, adding and subtracting people to our lives. Suresh, Ramesh and Ranjana got married and they in turn had children. By now our mother had also started coming to stay with each of us and so our association with Rajeswari and Ramesh became even less.

One day we heard Govind was no more. We all mourned him and as I write, I still feel the pangs of sorrow. He had drunk himself to death—a brilliant boy whom destiny completely ruined. Anyway, Rajeswari kept dropping in until one day our mother passed on.

A few months after that as I was still thinking of my mother and deeply mourning her loss (even though I myself am over 60 years of age now), Ramesh called. I answered his call with an affection I have never felt for him. He represented a connection with my past.

Ramesh was inconsolable. He told me Suresh had died in a road accident, leaving behind his wife and two children. Death and loss, which was what I was thinking about all the time, was almost like a real-life monster standing before me. I felt very bad for this young boy who must have been in his late 30s. I immediately sent Ramesh some money and told him I would take care of all the educational expenses of Suresh's children. Even my wife, who never wanted to have anything to do with that family, was upset. She started asking people for old clothes and even suggested that we keep Suresh's wife in our servants' quarter, if only for old times' sake.

I was touched by my wife's concern but Ramesh was not very enthusiastic. He said that the young widow was still coping and unable to take decisions. He said he would let me know soon.

Within a week, Ramesh called me again. This time he told me it was his mother. I knew Rajeswari was particularly fond of Suresh, her first-born child. Unable to take the grief, she had died. The poignancy of the situation robbed me of any pretensions of being "strong" or "pragmatic". I shut myself in my bedroom and cried. Not for Rajeswari, the bride who had had put up with all of Govind's shifting fortunes. Not for the fact that my mother would have mourned her deeply. Not for Ramesh. Not for anything. I do not know why I felt so disturbed. This is the attachment that the Buddha talked of, I reflected. She, Rajeswari, could not live without her son. So intense was her suffering that it took her life.

I started hearing philosophy podcasts. I tried very hard to come to terms with life and death. Mortality—that is the definition of human life. And for the first time, I folded my hands in prayer…

I had visions of Ramesh surrounded by four small kids (two of his own and two of his brother's) in that small hut of theirs. He also started sharing details of his grief with me. One message read, "Had to take the little one to the doctor to get a loose stomach treated." Another one read, "Suresh's son needs sports shoes for school."

Amidst all this there was also another problem. Ranjana had somehow got hold of the papers of the house that belonged to Govind. Read "house" as a small one-room structure that the government had allotted to them when they were evicted from a slum near our house. Now the fear was that Ranjana was transferring the house to her name. Rajeswari had asked me for help and advice. Could we get duplicate papers? Could we file a complaint? So many questions—and no possibility of mediation or talks. I had asked a lawyer who was my friend. This friend was well acquainted with the ways of the government. He was also generous and said he would do it free of cost. Now that Rajeswari had gone, I suggested that Ramesh should follow the matter. I told him several times that he should get death certificates, however painful the job may be. It would be required for all formalities, particularly for the house. I even asked my secretary to help Ramesh. But, Ramesh never answered his phone. To me, he kept saying he would do it soon, but before he could take one step, another tragedy struck.

That is when Ramesh called me to say his wife had died. Three deaths in a matter of two months! I went mad with grief. I did not know how to console him. Why do such things also happen? I asked as I cried. I sent him money for the funeral and for the first time involved all my siblings and sent Ramesh a lump sum in addition. My wife was gracious enough to give our savings for our trip to Europe.

Two days later, I went to my lawyer friend's house. My wife had shooed me out of the home saying going out would help me raise my spirits. I decided to go his house because it had been a long time since I had met him. Members of his family had got Covid. One after another his children, wife and he had been infected. So they had been practically inaccessible. My friend had got it first and been the last to recover in the sense that he still had a relentless cough and weakness. He had lost weight.

He was happy to see me…it was the first interaction he was having after many months, he commented. It was on the tip of my tongue to tell him about Rajeswari's family but I refrained for I did not want to burden a man in such a condition with tales of sorrow.

It was a pleasant winter's day in Delhi and I was sitting in his balcony. We discussed a little before we decided to have tea because that involved the "dangerous" act of taking off our masks to prevent infections!

He brought some delectable *samosa*s with the tea. "They are homemade," he announced proudly. And slowly but surely he started cracking jokes…showing that his spirit was still intact. He always has been a treasure house of husband–wife jokes. “The husband got Aladdin’s lamp,” he was saying. “Oh what will you ask for?” asked his wife dreamily, as she looked at him holding the lamp....”

Before he could finish, the gate rattled and the doorbell rang. “Oh, no! Do not mind my saying that, but here she is again...she comes every Sunday,” he said as he looked out to see who had rung the doorbell.

“Who?” I asked as I seemed to be implicated in that statement. I gently pushed aside the leaves of the potted plant blocking my view of the surroundings and peeped out.

There stood Rajeswari, in flesh and blood. Suresh was parking his scooter....

Framed Picture

"Oh, you look so lovely!" exclaimed Shyamala, picking up the photograph on the mantelpiece. "Look at Chithappa…," she began, peering into the picture of her father's younger brother. Lakshmi choked.

"Ayyo, what happened, are you okay, Chithi?" cried Shyamala running towards Lakshmi, her aunt.

"Oh, I am okay, just swallowed water the wrong way, I think," replied Lakshmi with a smile, reaching out to caress her niece. Shyamala smiled back. A tall and pretty girl, Shyamala was in her early 20s.

"*Yen di*, Shyamala," called out Lalitha, Shyamala's mother, "Show me the picture also."

"Manni, let her eat," interjected Lakshmi wanting to draw her sister-in-law's attention away from the photograph. "The *bonda*s are going cold. I just made them so that they are hot and crisp for her." (Bondas are deep-fried snacks made of potatoes).

"Thank you, Chithi!" exclaimed Shyamala, "You are so kind. It's been a long time since I had *bonda*s. They are really yummy."

"When did you take that photograph, Lakshmi?" asked Lalitha with her eyes narrowed, trying to get a better look at the picture. She was sitting on the floor and the mantelpiece on which the framed photograph sat was a little distance away, at the end of the room.

"I do not remember, Manni, maybe last year…or two years back…Will you have coffee or Horlicks?"

"I will have Horlicks," said Lalitha. "Before you go into the kitchen, give me the photograph," added Lalitha.

"What is the hurry, Manni…I will give it to you. But first drink your Horlicks, you look very weak. How is your knee pain nowadays?"

"Oh! What to tell you…my maid has not been coming to work here for more than two weeks now." With that, the photograph was completely forgotten and Lakshmi relaxed.

Shyamala helped her bring the Horlicks and coffee to the hall, which was what they called their living room. The red floor with Mangalore tiles was shining and uncluttered. There were two rosewood chairs, large and comfortable, in one corner. They had cane woven on the seats and backs. Between them was a round table, also made of rosewood, which had piles of newspaper and dust on it. They rarely sat in the living room. When her husband was alive he would always sit there to drink his coffee. Now Venky did, sometimes.

Lakshmi sat down on the floor, opposite Lalitha, and the conversation moved from her maid to her neighbour who had three house helps…the front door was open. Cool breeze was wafting in now that it was past noon.

"When will Venky come?" asked Shyamala.

"I told him you are coming. He said he would come as early as possible," said Lakshmi. Venky was her son, her eldest child. She had four daughters born after him. Two of them were married. The other two were at their different institutions for studies.

And so their conversation went on till they saw Venky's cycle swerve into the gate. Shyamala called out to him and he responded as enthusiastically. After Venky came in and the greetings were over, Lalitha said, "Venky, give me that photograph…I have been asking for it for so long…your mother is too shy to show it to me. She does not even tell me when she took it."

Shyamala got up in a huff and said, "Here, look at it to your heart's content…you are such a nag…" and gave her mother the photograph.

"What is this? Subramaniam has closed his eyes…." Lalitha was saying.

Shyamala piped in, "Amma, the photographer caught him when he was blinking in the glare of the lights."

Lakshmi sat down. She thought she would faint. She could not listen to anything anymore.

Whenever he drew her close to him, she would ask him, "*Yen na*, shall we go tomorrow?" (*Yen na* was a customary way of addressing the husband because a wife he could not call him by his name).

"*Podi ashadu*," he would say dismissively. (Come on, silly girl). The rest of the conversation was hushed out by quickening breaths.

And then she would get pregnant—she would not ask him that question till she delivered. Five children had been born so that had considerably reduced the number of times the question had been posed.

Lakshmi was very beautiful. Of course, most people thought so because she was of fair skin and in Tamil Nadu, this asset was greatly admired. But, fairness was not only why Lakshmi was considered beautiful. She had very sharp features, a defined jawline, almond-shaped eyes, a very gentle expression, and such full lips. There was a certain honesty and sincerity that shone through her personality. She got married to Subramaniam when she was only 15. Subramaniam had been studying law then. He was 22 years of age. His father, Sankaran, was a leading advocate of the town and his brother, Chandrasekhar, five years older, had also studied law and was now working with his father. Subramaniam too would join the firm when he finished studying.

Subramaniam was a very nice man, loving to his wife, kind to his children (as they came along), obedient to his parents, hardworking as a lawyer and so on. He had only one problem: he did not deem Lakshmi's question worth answering. He was dark as night, had white teeth that shone in the dark, with a beautiful smile and infectious laughter. As a lawyer, he helped people and so was very popular. More popular than his brother, Lakshmi would have told you.

When Lakshmi got married, Lalitha had been her closest friend and support. Her mother-in-law was more or less always sick and the conversations with her were more in the nature of care-giving. Lalitha was five years older than her. She already had two babies by then, two boys. Lakshmi was very helpful in looking after them. They had a cook who would turn out elaborate meals according to everyone's liking. Lalitha and Lakshmi served the members of the household, which would often mean cousins, aunts and uncles too. The two sisters-in-law would confide in and take advice from each other.

One day, Lakshmi told her sister-in-law that she happened to see a *Woman and Home* magazine in Miss Daniel's hands. Miss Daniel had taught her English at school. On the cover of the magazine was the picture of a couple…the woman was sitting on a chair and her husband was standing behind her with his left hand placed lovingly on her left shoulder.

"Manni, I want a picture like this," Lakshmi told her sister-in-law.

"Forget it, stupid girl. This is India. Can you have a picture taken alone with your husband? Never. They are foreigners… in their country, they have no shame. Husbands and wives even hold hands in public."

"What is wrong in that, Manni?" asked Lakshmi.

"*Ayyo*! Don't ask that. It is certainly not our culture," Lalitha replied.

"That is so romantic, Manni," sighed Lakshmi. "I have kept one of my wedding saris to wear if and when we take a picture like that…." Lakshmi kept dreaming. No one photographed weddings when she got married. So she had no picture of the two of them.

Even though Lalitha and Lakshmi were great friends, Lalitha did not let her forget that she was the senior. For example, if her father-in-law bought them two saris and offered them to Lakshmi because she was younger, Lakshmi would catch Lalitha looking at her.

"Oh! Let Manni choose…she knows what is best for me." Lakshmi would dither while Lalitha would choose the sari for her. As years went by, they had less time for each other. Their children took all their time. Lalitha had seven of them. A rivalry between the children and so between the mothers also started raising its head.

By now her father-in-law had divided his extensive land into two and the brothers began to live independently. It took three minutes to walk from one house to the other and this gave the women their privacy, which they enjoyed.

Now Lakshmi's question came out in the open and while he sat looking into his files and the children were studying or playing, she would ask, "*Yen na*, can we go tomorrow?"

Sometimes he would pretend not to hear. On other times he would gesture to her to keep quiet. That gesture, if put in words, would read, "People will laugh at me if I say I want to take a picture with my wife… what will the world say?"

Everyone in the town knew Subramaniam. It was true that it would not remain a secret if they went to the studio to take a picture. There was only one studio…and whoever went there was the talk of the town. Often the printed photograph would be displayed in the shop window before the family collected it.

Meanwhile, Lakshmi's children were indeed growing up and so the question got a little lost at times. Her two daughters, Kamakshi and Meenakshi, had got married one after another as there was only a difference of a year between them. They were barely 15 when they got married. Lakshmi was in her early 30s when she became a mother-in-law.

Venky was a responsible brother, one year older to Kamakshi, the eldest of the daughters. There was a gap of three years between Meenakshi and Amla and Vimala. Then Lakshmi had lost a child. Amla was now 12 years old and so the Subramaniams had some time before they started looking for a groom for her.

Venky had told his parents he was not going to get married in a hurry. His father got married when he was 22 years of age, so he asked for at least that much time. Venky's father agreed for he wanted his son to take over his practice.

Venky's friends used to come home and Lakshmi and Subramaniam would keep scanning them to see if any of them would be suitable for their next son-in-law.

One day, Venky's friend Pichu came home with a good-looking boy who wore a turban. "The family of my friend are Sikhs and live in northern India, Punjab," said Venky introducing him. "He has come with his father. They are making a film on Ooty." This was the first time the family had seen a turbaned Sikh. They were tenants at Pichu's house; therefore, Pichu and Harvinder used to come often to play with Venky.

Lalitha told Lakshmi to be careful of north Indian boys… "Your daughters…," she said meaningfully. Subramaniam also heard Lalitha's warning and started becoming very protective of his daughters. But, Venky liked Harvinder. "Amma, be nice to him. He misses his mother," Venky would tell Lakshmi. He would not only insist that Lakshmi feed the boy a good meal, whenever he came, but also pack snacks for him to take home. Lakshmi used to feel Venky overdid it sometimes.

While these thoughts were filling their minds, Lakshmi asked her husband her favourite question again, half in play. Her daughter Vimala said, "Amma, but we have a picture with Thatha Patti (the grandparents) and everyone else..." Then Subramaniam glared at her. That night he told her, "With grown-up daughters you want to take a picture with your husband...they will get wrong ideas...let them get married."

Lakshmi replied, "But, we have absolutely no picture of our family...the one Vimala was talking about is in the family album and Manni would not part with it for life."

Subramaniam dismissed her with a wave of his hand and said, "Can I have a little coffee?"

Only Venky would look at Lakshmi with big understanding eyes. His mother was only 16 years older than him. He was 17 now and she was 33. She had a right to have some fun, he felt. He even suggested to his dad that he take her desire a little seriously. His father had playfully patted his head and walked off.

The tipping point came when Lalitha's son got married and his in-laws had a photographer at the wedding. Then Lalitha posed with her husband as Lakshmi had always wanted to, and the photographer took a nice picture. Worse, she called Lakshmi and showed her the photograph saying, "I have always wanted a picture like this."

"But Manni, I told you what I want," said Lakshmi. No one heard her. Everyone was busy admiring Lalitha and Chandrasekhar's picture. Lakshmi's eyes smarted with tears.

That evening, Subramaniam appeased her. "See, now it has become simple for us. When Anna (brother) and Manni can take a picture like that, so can we. When Venky gets us a camera, we will pose," he said jovially. That meant at Venky's wedding, "we too will pose". But, Lakshmi did not hide her pique. Venky somehow felt burdened. He alone could fulfil his mother's wish.

Venky was 19 when his father got fever one day. Amla had just been married off. The fatigue caused by the wedding celebrations had not yet worn off. Everyone felt Subramaniam had overstrained himself. Lakshmi made the usual *kashayam* (herbal medication) to reduce his fever. That did not have any effect, so the doctor was called. Treatment began but in a day, his condition worsened and things looked bad. Suddenly the house, which had been bustling with joy, was in the grip of fear and sorrow. On the third morning when Venky had just left for college, Muthu, their house help came running behind him saying, "Amma is calling you…urgently." Venky knew what had happened. But he did not turn back. He cycled furiously on.

"Where is Venky, Muthu?" asked Lakshmi tearfully.

"Amma, I told him, but he cycled away even faster." said Muthu in between sobs.

"Go call Anna and Manni," said Lakshmi between sobs to Muthu. As Muthu was leaving, Venky rushed in. Along with him was the turbaned Sikh boy, Harvinder.

"Muthu, first go to school and fetch Vimala," said Venky. He almost pushed Muthu out of the door and shut it.

He dragged his crying mother inside. "No, no, Venky, how can I? Stop it, Venky," Lakshmi was heard pleading from inside. Venky was saying, "Amma, this is the only chance … please cooperate…no, Harvinder will not tell anyone…he speaks only Hindi…he is leaving for Punjab tomorrow." Her heart bled, but she decided to think for a moment of that teasing smile on her husband's face whenever she mentioned her desire for a photograph.

She picked up her red sari and wore it. She clasped diamonds in her ears, diamonds around her neck, diamonds on her nose. She wore a big red *kumkum* (a red dot on the forehead worn by married women) and Venky brought her the jasmine flowers from the *puja* room.

Venky and Harvinder had made Subramaniam's body sit up on the chair. They struggled to put a coat on him… one arm could not be put in, but they camouflaged it. They tied his usual turban and even put the traditional mark on his forehead. "Come Amma, come, come," Venky yelled. Lakshmi stood beside her husband, while the Sikh boy clicked many pictures…maybe two or three. And the two of them were caught for posterity.

No one knew how much effort it took for Venky and Harvinder. Harvinder had returned to Punjab. He had developed the pictures in his hometown and then sent them.

That is why Lalitha was seeing it now for the first time. That is why no one knew when the photographs had been taken.

In one, Lakshmi put her hand over his shoulder…as Harvinder clicked. That was the picture Lalitha was peering closely at. Would she see that one sleeve was resting on a listless arm?

Lakshmi could not bear the tension. She saw herself in the mirror. Today, she stood in a white sari, with a shaved head, wearing no blouse since widows were not supposed to. Would Lalitha discover that she had posed with her dead husband?

Fated Strokes

"Bindu, Bindu!" my husband was screaming from the living room, "Come here, we have some great news." I hurried there, thinking maybe our children had announced that they would be visiting or if we had found a new discount for our holiday plans. "Renuka's daughter is getting married," he said.

"Yes, I know. Is that why you made me come all this way?" I asked, a little irritated. Renuka is my sister-in-law, Mohan's sister. We had already spoken to Renuka and her husband. I was even doing some wedding shopping for her. She lives in Chennai.

"No Bindu, there is even better news. We just figured out that Renuka's daughter is marrying your cousin Sarita's husband's nephew."

"Oh? How did you find that out?" I asked.

He went on to tell me how he was speaking to his brother who described the family with whom their sister had fixed this alliance. "The youngsters were classmates and then even worked in the same organisation...." Even as Mohan was describing all this, I was beginning to feel some discomfort. The inevitable came, "So when we go, we will meet Sarita also...I have never met her though you speak so much about her. Let us go on next Wednesday."

I was too numb to speak. I had looked forward to this wedding, the first of the next-generation weddings. But now...a fear gripped me. After all these years I did not think this situation would crop up. "Why Wednesday? The wedding is only on the following Thursday...why should we go so early? Anyway, I do not know if I will get leave," I muttered. Anything to avoid going to the wedding.

"You will not attend Renuka's daughter's wedding?" asked my husband, shocked.

"I will, I will," I said and walked out of the room. My cousin Sarita and I were close friends. We had been inseparable. When Sarita got married, I was in the middle of my final examinations and so could not attend her wedding. When I got married, she was expecting her first child, which is why she could not attend. This way providence and a little of my will kept us apart all these years. Another factor that helped, was that her husband was in the Merchant Navy and so was forever overseas. When he came home, the family could not get enough of him so they did not plan any extended family visits then. I once met Sarita at another cousin's wedding. She had come alone and so had I. We had a good time together. She kept talking of how our families should get together and all that, but I gave one excuse after another. Mohan is very busy with work. Mohan's parents are there. Mohan is travelling…name it and I had used these excuses at one time or other. So, all these years, about 29 in all, we had not met. Now the meeting seemed unavoidable.

My parents had attended Sarita's wedding and my mother had come back with a photograph of the newly wedded couple. I was eager to see who my dear cousin was marrying. In those days we had to wait for the photographer to process the negative and give us a picture to see. So, I had to wait for almost a week for my parents to return to see the picture. Of course, Sarita had made a trunk call and I had said hello to her husband, but that was only briefly. His voice sounded familiar, but I did not think more about it till I saw the picture.

I was shocked and almost cried on seeing Sarita with her husband, Brahma. I knew Brahma. In fact, we knew each other. Not only did he know me, but he knew one of my secrets, the only one. We both studied in the Delhi University though he was doing his Master's when I had just joined for my undergraduation course. I was studying in Miranda House and he was in Hindu College. There used to be a corner shop at the end of the lane behind our college and I used to sneak out there because I wanted a *bidi*. Yes, I would smoke in secret. No one knew, not even my friends. Once in a while my friends would say I smelt of smoke…I would say it must be the smell that rubbed off from someone in the bus. I had to keep this habit away from my parents. It was a common feeling that only *bigdi huwi ladkiyan* (immoral girls) smoked. So, my parents would have thrown a fit. I had my grandparents also staying with us. It would have become a scandal that I would never have been able to face. Even cigarettes may not have been so abysmal as the *bidi*.

I used to buy them from a shop where the shopkeeper was a young boy. I would sneak into the small kiosk, sit down there, smoke and then emerge. This shop used to be less frequented by people because it was not on the main road. Also, the boy who manned the shop was the nephew of the owner. The owner would come to the shop only after lunch and all the peons and sweepers would gather here for a tete-tete with a *bidi* only then. The young boy would begin making *chai* in the afternoon and the owner would bring baskets full of *samosa*s and bread *pakora*s for sale.

Before one in the afternoon, the shop was deserted. Another person who frequented the shop was Brahma. Initially, I tried to hide from him but soon it became impossible. Almost every day I would meet him at least once. (I would visit the shop about three times between eight in the morning and half past one in the afternoon). Soon we got talking. Brahma asked me my name which I never told him lest he mention it to somebody and my secret was let out of the bag. Brahma also liked *bidi*s but preferred cigarettes. He did not have to hide it from anyone since a boy was "allowed" to smoke. In fact, it was stylish for a man to smoke. He was amused to find I liked smoking a *bidi*.

"But why?" he asked me, "Is it because cigarettes are more expensive?"

At first I did not answer but when we met day after day, we got talking one day and I said, "We have a gardener at home. He comes to work with his wife. They both sit down to take a break and share a *bidi*. I have often asked them what that was and they laughed it off, saying they were renewing their energy. One day, the wife of the gardener gave me a puff. "Don't tell your mother that I gave you a whiff," she said. Initially, I didn't much like it but the thrill of running into the garden, waiting for a lone moment and taking the *bidi* from her was getting more and more exciting every day. Soon I was hooked on it."

We also spoke of other things. What he was studying, what I was studying. What our fathers did. How big our family was and so on. He also called me a coward because I was not able to be open with my liking. A hypocrite, he said one day. Another time he said that if I was ashamed of doing what I was, I should stop. I tried to shut all his advice away from my ears. He was right. Anyway, I was guilty but I felt I would stop once I stopped going to college…so I thought I was a temporary hypocrite. We all err temporarily… so it is okay.

"It is not. You cannot give it up so easily," he said…but these conversations were far and few between. Most of the time we had more interesting topics to discuss. I still did not tell him my name so used to call me Bidi. Once when he was driving past our college on a motorbike, he saw me walking with a friend of mine. "Hey, Bidi," he yelled.

"Wow, that is a smart guy," said my friend, while I was almost in tears.

"I don't know him, *yaar*," I lied.

"But he called you by your name," she said and I froze.

"He said B.D.... Bindu Doraiswami..." she continued...I started breathing again. Yes, they were my initials.

This must have gone on for about a year. I don't know how it stopped...one day he didn't come to the shop and soon I too could not go there as often as I used to. I graduated and once in a while would still steal a puff from my gardener's wife. Then somehow, life got busy and I did not miss it. One of the reasons was perhaps that my grandfather whom I loved dearly fell ill and all my energies shifted to worrying about him. I was also his favourite grandchild so I appointed myself as his caregiver and that obsession took over me.

All was well till I saw the picture of the wedding that my mother showed me and found Brahma had married my very own cousin! He would definitely tell his wife about me when he met me and she would tell her mother who would tell my mother. The train of thoughts was killing me. So you see, I had no other option but to stay away from Brahma. Now it has been 29 years since Sarita got married. About 27 and a half since I got married. Would Renuka's daughter's wedding ruin my peaceful life?

My husband was an ethical man who had very strong views on the good and the bad. There were never any grey areas for him. He would not be able to understand that I had taken a fancy to smoking and had actually indulged in it. That it lasted a short time and that it hardly means anything to me now, were arguments that would fall on deaf ears. He would immediately label me as "immoral" and then add on accusations like, "That is why our daughter is always rebelling. You have not given her the right values." Or, "How do you expect to control your son when you yourself cheated your parents and had no qualms about smoking?" I could imagine different ways in which we would fight and all that could happen to me thereafter. My parents too would not be on my side. My brother's wife never liked me and now she would say, "I told you so," to my brother. What would I do?

In the coming days, Sarita called one day, very excited. 'Finally, we will have a nice time together. I will meet your husband," said Sarita.

"Why, what about yours? Is Brahma not coming?" I asked hopefully.

"Oh no! He will be there…wish you had met him earlier," she said a little wistfully, I thought. I went through angst and more angst. I had imagined at least a hundred different ways in which Mohan could react to this revelation. Not one of them was positive. I could not even imagine him saying, "That's okay. I would love to hear about your experience," or some such thing.

I had bizarre ideas of wearing a *burkha* or a bandage around my face saying I had got burnt…with all this you can understand the state of my mind. But I did change my hairstyle, opted for burgundy instead of black for my hair and even got my nose pierced and wore a nose pin…hoping all this would change my appearance somewhat. And, for the first time I was glad to think that I had also aged.

The day came when we packed and left for Chennai where the wedding was taking place. I was feeling sick. We went straight to my sister-in-law's house. "Sarita has invited us for tea this evening," said Renuka. "She can't wait to meet you. I am so glad the groom's family is known to your family…." I was not listening to Renuka. Another three hours of joy was all I had.

That evening, we went for tea. Sarita came out and hugged me. She was very nice to Mohan. She led us into the living room. "Brahma, see who is here. My dear cousin Bindu," called out Sarita cheerfully. I could barely take a step forward.

I saw a man on a wheelchair. Sarita hugged him and introduced us. "He had a stroke three months ago," whispered Sarita as she continued with the introductions. Brahma had not changed much, except for the scars his recent illness had left on him. He seemed to be peering into my face. I looked the other way. Mohan greeted him and Brahma responded weakly. Then suddenly, with his face lighting up, he said, "Bidi." It was like a recognition. Then he said. "Bidi…Bidi" pointing to me with a twinkle in his eyes.

I thought the earth would cave and swallow me. Sarita looked embarrassed.

"Come on, Brahma," said Sarita with a short laugh. "What is making you think about a *bidi* now. It is time for your juice."She called out to her maid and said, "It is time for *ayya*'s juice. Please bring it." Sitting down beside Brahma, Sarita said, "Brahma, I will just chat with them for some time…you seem tired. You rest and I will be back soon."

His eyes were still looking at me quizzically. Slowly, as Sarita's words made sense, he looked down.

Sarita led us out of the room to serve us tea in the dining room. "The stroke has impacted his memory…he is disjointed in his speech…sorry about that," she said with an apologetic laugh.

As I sipped my tea, I could see Brahma in the other room, sitting hopelessly, head tilted to the side. The room was quiet and lonely, his drooping figure formed a silent silhouette against the fading light. If I had said, "Hey, Brahma, you recognised me! Do you remember that lane?" Would that have helped him recover?

I just left him to be "insane"…to save my life.

Roses *are* Forever

General Rajan stretched his legs under the table as he sat in his plush office. He looked at the clock. It was a quarter to one. Time ticked slower these days, he thought, as he picked up the glass of water from the table. The Air Chief Marshall's death had upset him, though he was very careful not to show it. When his wife spoke about it, he even told her it was silly of her to go on and on like that. "We all have to go sometime, then why all this fuss?" he had shouted. But he knew why. He also knew why he was upset.

He was upset because it struck him that this was just the way he would have liked to go too! He was not afraid of the end. He was afraid he would live too long, go into a living oblivion with only guilt and regrets as his companions. And ever since this thought had struck him, Gautam Rajan was just going over and over his life.

He had done well at his job, had devoted his life to it and had been rewarded too. He had dreamt of being a General of a nation's Armed Forces. His dreams had come true and were followed by medals.

Rajan grew thoughtful as he smoothed his moustache. His wife Anjali had never liked it and had always felt the moustache made him look like a rogue. Not respectable. "Bah!" said the General to himself. If a General is not respectable, then who is? Sometimes Anjali had fixed notions and no amount of reasoning could make her change her mind. Even though she was a scientist, he thought wryly. She was a scientist and a very good one at that. His expression mellowed as he thought of her. She had large eyes, a very clear complexion and was good-looking in a simple way.

Anjali had tried to involve him in all her projects, sought his help, even his guidance, but he had not heeded her. He wanted her to be a normal wife, to dress with care and attend or throw parties and generally be happy-go-lucky rather than sit all day pouring over botanical books and getting excited about some vague plant in Australia.

One aspect that was a real source of pride to him was that she maintained the garden really well. In fact, one of his commanding officers had been so impressed by his garden that his opinion of Rajan had gone up. Anjali grumbled when the flowers were cut, but Rajan made it a point to see that a few flowers and plants from his garden were regularly sent to the commanding officer's house.

Rajan sweated even as he thought of it now. His whole career could have been different but for the gardens in his life. Thank God Anjali was a botanist, not a physicist or something. But of late he had begun to feel Anjali deserved more. He should have shown more interest in her work. Did she think he was dumb? He wasn't. It was just that his career was important and demanded all his time and thought.

Today when he thought of his son, a professor of anthropology, serious, stable, greatly in demand in India as well as in universities abroad and his daughter in Philadelphia, an author of many books and a student of sociology there, he felt a little left out. What would they think of him? A frivolous nitwit? Rajan winced. They all loved him very much, he knew, but surely as a father he should have given more to his children? Today if he closed his book of life, in harness, maybe many dignitaries would tell the rest of the world of his qualities as a General and then maybe his family would have pride in him, something he felt he failed to impress on them so far.

The door opened and his staff officer clicked to attention. It was time for General Rajan to go home. The thought of home sent ripples through his mind and he was not sure what he wanted.

On the way he stopped to buy some roses and somehow his heart felt lighter. Anjali would be waiting.

Perhaps it was time to turn his mind from guns to roses....

Once Upon a Flight

For the last time before leaving the restroom, Rohini looked at herself in the mirror, adjusted her top, slung her bag on her shoulder and walked out, pulling a tissue out of the holder as she went out into the departure lounge. They would announce boarding very soon. The flight was already two hours late. Now the announced time of departure was four-fifteen in the morning. She could well have got a little sleep and come to the airport by two in the morning. But no, she was here by 11 in the night. with her husband, mother and father in tow.

Her parents had come to drop her off at the airport because the occasion was special. She was going to New Jersey for her nephew's, her brother's son's wedding. He was marrying an American. Since her parents were 85 and 90, they were not confident of undertaking such a long journey. Rohini's husband could not get leave. Therefore, Rohini was on her way to New Jersey alone.

She sat down in a chair in the waiting area and put her bag in the empty chair next to her. Crossing her legs, she leant back, letting her head rest on the back of the chair. Even though she had wanted to travel light, her bag had become heavy. She did not have much in it. What made the bag heavy was not the extra shirt, nor the book that she had brought to read on the flight. Nor was it the talisman her mother had insisted she carry for safe travelling. "No danger will come to you," her mother had said.

Rohini had laughed and said, "Amma, I am going on a flight not to a jungle."

Her mother had maintained her serious expression saying, "Flights nowadays are equally hazardous. Look at how many security checks you have to undergo."

Rohini's bag was heavy because of her diary. It was hardbound and thick.

"Why do you want to carry that in your hand baggage?" her daughter had asked and her husband had shrugged his shoulders as though to show how helpless he was in the face of extreme unreasonableness.

"How much will you write on the flight, Mama? Take a small pad," she had suggested.

"I am carrying the bag. Then let me have the freedom to decide what I take in it," Rohini had replied sharply.

As her eyes fell on the lady sitting in the last seat of the facing row, she knew why she had opted to wear trousers and a long shirt. That lady was wearing a bright red *salwar kameez* and Hawaii slippers, hair tied back; she looked what one would describe as a *behenji* (an unsophisticated country bumpkin). Rohini's glance took in four more ladies, older than her and the other two of her age, attired in jeans and *kurtis*. Looking at them, she thought to herself wryly, "It is our shot at being Westernised."

Even among those who wore the same kind of clothes, there was a hierarchy of smartness. Those who had short hair and firm steps on block heels presented a picture of confidence, overshadowing those with long hair which had to be made into a bun or plaited. Rohini belonged to the second category, with fuzzy hair that insisted on telling the world that all her jabs at modernity were superficial. She would have preferred to wear a sari, but it was not so comfortable on long flights and in the US, her brother could never understand why she made such a big deal of Indian clothes and would insist she wear trousers like everybody else. If Rohini was ever asked to describe herself, she would say she had a loose heavy body clad in aspiring clothes.

"Okay, okay, just trying to help you," said Meera, her 22-year-old daughter. She was working in a multinational company after her post-graduation.

Rohini pulled out her notebook at the airport, clicked open her pen and looked around. Maybe her claim to fame may begin right here, on this chair in the departure lounge, of the Indira Gandhi International Airport, New Delhi!

Rohini aspired to be a writer. To be more precise, a bestselling author. In fact, that was the password to all her email accounts. Wherever she saw the name of J.K. Rowling on the bookshelves in shops, she would visualise her own face and name on a book and place it on the same shelf.

Rohini Taran. Her dreams were not in the air as she had written many books. One was lost by the publisher—it had been handwritten and was lost forever. The other she herself rejected. Yet another lay incomplete. However, she had completed the fourth one.

She had written it painstakingly. Corrected it. Rewritten it. Printed it out. Prepared a synopsis. By that time she was working on a computer and so had copies of her work. She had as many sets ready with sample chapters and the storyline neatly presented in a couple of paragraphs. Adding her curriculum vitae to that she went to many publishers. No one responded. Those who did, sent the standard letter that they regretted their inability to publish the work but wished her all the best. These letters made Rohini want to claw the publisher. No, she was not apologetic for the violence in her thoughts, she felt 10 times more than the word meant to any reader.

Then one day, a publisher agreed to meet her. She was excited. She got a facial done, bought a fancy file cover for her manuscript and was all set. Life was going to change she thought and wished she could lose just a couple of kilograms before fame tagged on. The publisher turned out to be her father's student who gave her the same advice but in more refined words. He told her to write her stories with the diaspora in mind.

It was then that her brother called to invite her. Rohini was not too keen because somehow many years of living apart had made her less communicative with her brother. His wife, Maria, was Mexican. Since she was pleasant and cheerful, Rohini got on better with her. But she did not feel like going alone but thought, "Is God giving me just one more chance to become famous?"

From the next day, Rohini was busy booking tickets, buying clothes and very eager to go on her flight—to everyone's surprise. Her secret, she held very close to her heart.

She caressed her notebook and thought she should write something. She put down the date and wrote pompously "En route to NY". She looked around, aware that she should be serious and focused. A writer had to be alert to every detail. "You never know, I may find an important character here," she thought.

She saw a middle-aged Indian couple, the man in a T-shirt and wearing the expression most Indian men living abroad and prospering wear, which said, "I have arrived. Have a house worth 1-2 million dollars. Daughter in Yale, son in Princeton and wife, oh she is not like the average Indian one tied to the kitchen. We are all equal there you know and I even do the dishes for her. She works in...."

"How are you sure they think all this?" Taran would ask when she told him about such observations. "Maybe that is the expression he was born with."

"All of them? Born with the same expression?" Rohini would ask and Taran would decide his wife was allowed her imagination and not argue further.

The wife of the man Rohini was sketching in words, was obviously educated. She was not the one who wore trousers, a hip shirt with her *mangal sutra* and *sindoor* to emphasise her status of a married woman. This one was reading Barack Obama's *The Audacity of Hope*. She had a clean face, hair in a short boy-cut and a thin chain around her neck. She wore jeans and a black T-shirt with a long shirt over it. She was comfortably plump but carried the weight as a placard of her prosperity. A solitaire glistened on her fingers. Look for details, the writer in Rohini told her, and yet Rohini could not see her ears for her hair was long enough on the sides to cover them.

A young couple sat with two children. One was running around and ever so busy and the other was sleeping in the pushchair. The husband and wife were pouring over a Fodor's guide to London. They were white-skinned.

Two young men sat at the end of the same row of seats where Rohini was. One was bald and thin, the other of average height and rather nondescript. The bald one was reading the back cover of a book …Rohini peered closer, it was not Urdu, not Persian…must be Hebrew she thought… Ha! What a discovery! But not enough to spin a story around, anyway.

The flight's departure time was announced and Rohini had to abandon her perceptive study of human beings in the airport. She could continue it on her flight, though.

As Rohini took her seat, 42A, and snuggled close to the window, she found the meek-looking "country bumpkin" take the seat beside her. Obviously a Sardarini, the Sikh lady would not smile, did not even look at her. She had a blue and red airbag which seemed heavy. Rohini offered to put it up in the bin for her, but the lady refused to let her help and just pushed it under the seat in front of her. It jutted out a little but she put her feet on it and that kind of settled it.

When the announcements began about the flight being ready to take off, she suddenly turned to Rohini and asked in semi-Punjabi, "Is this not the flight going to London?"

"Yes," said Rohini. "It will stop in London. Are you going there?"

She nodded vigorously in the affirmative and asked "*Vahan kitni der rukegi*?" (How long will it stop there?).

"I don't really know. I think about four hours. The aircraft is refuelled there," replied Rohini.

"Please tell me when to get down, so that I don't miss London," said the woman who seemed to be in her mid-30s. Punjabi women have that glow and health about them even if their family legacy was not looks, but this lady had none of those attributes. Or maybe the fear writ large on her face was hiding anything else that might be present. Her skin was sallow and dry. She had a sharp nose and thin lips. Her hair was tightly braided into a single plait that fell just below her shoulder. She wore absolutely no jewellery, not even earrings. Around her neck she wore a black thread and around her wrist was a red thread. She smelt of rancid butter.

"Oh! Don't worry! There's plenty of time. The crew will tell you," said Rohini, pointing to the airhostess. She realised that this was the first time the lady was on an aircraft. In fact, it was the first time she had stepped out of Bhatinda, a small town in Punjab, the lady told her after much cajoling and also said her name was Guddi.

As the aircraft leapt into the air, Guddi clenched her fists, tore a piece of newspaper and put it into her mouth. Rohini was a little taken aback. She called to her, tapped her on her forearm. But she refused to hear Rohini or look at her. For quite some time, till the aircraft had completed its ascent, she sat still and tight, not leaning back. She was wearing a brown shawl which looked new, but its colour was rather depressing. She was clutching a brown handbag placed on her lap and continuing to sit absolutely straight. When drinks were served, she refused. When food was offered, she vehemently shook her head.

"But you must have something," said Rohini, feeling Guddi's tension. "What are you worried about? Nothing can happen to you in the aircraft. We will all help you. And when you get down, somebody will be there to receive you. Who are you going to visit in London?"

Maybe she was worried about being hijacked, mused Rohini.

Slowly, after very obviously weighing the pros and cons of confiding in a stranger, Guddi said, "My husband." She fished out a picture of their wedding from her bag and pointed to the man.

"Oh! What fun!" exclaimed Rohini, "I am sure you will have a lovely time. He must be eagerly waiting for you."

Guddi held Rohini's hand and pressing it tightly said, "You think so? I have not seen him since I got married—six years ago."

Rohini's heart sank suddenly.

"I have been living with my brother for all this time. He said I had to go to my husband's house and so is sending me over. He must also be tired of another mouth to feed," Guddi was saying.

"But did your husband not call for you? Was he not talking on the telephone with you? Maybe he did not get leave from office to come to India," Rohini said, trying to sound hopeful.

With a blank expression that showed she had not heard Rohini at all, Guddi continued, "He has not replied to a single letter from me. I have not seen him since he left the day after the wedding…"

"Then are you sure he will receive you? Will you be able to recognise him?" asked Rohini, very concerned.

She nodded. Rohini wondered if that was a yes or a no.

"Somebody will come. My Taoji's son is here." (The father's elder brother is referred to as Taoji). "My brother has told him to take me to my husband if he does not come to receive me. My husband has also been informed…but there has been no response from him. Maybe the number we have is old…maybe he has changed house…I am sure he must be fine or else his family would have told us. They, too, have not got any news from him since our wedding…"

By now Rohini was so worried hearing this woman's story that she could no longer bear it. "Eat something or else how will you manage? You will feel hungry," urged Rohini.

"No. I am too nervous. I may throw up, if I do," she replied and suddenly went silent again. All through the seven hours when Rohini had dozed off, watched a movie and read some chapters of a book, Guddi had sat upright staring at the front without blinking. "Would you like to go to the washroom?" Rohini had asked, "I can take you." Guddi had shaken her head sideways to say no.

As the flight landed, Rohini told her it was time for her to get down. Guddi picked up her heavy blue and red bag and walked to the exit. She turned to look at Rohini and nod goodbye. There was a knot in Rohini's stomach. Then suddenly she came back, "Where should I go?" she asked, "will they be waiting with my suitcase?"

Rohini went up to the airhostess. She explained Guddi's predicament and asked if someone could help her. All the time she found an irritating man trying to eavesdrop on their conversation. His hair was thick and brown. He was tall, clean-shaven, in a blue shirt which had dark blue fish motifs and jeans. Something about him made Rohini get goose pimples. But that, thought Rohini, was so wrong of her because he turned out to be very helpful. He stepped forward and said, "Can I help? I am getting down here and I can escort her out...my wife is coming to receive me," he said as though to assuage my doubts. "I speak Punjabi well and so should be able to render some assistance to a fellow Indian..." He began speaking to Guddi. Initially, Guddi did not look his way and she kept replying while looking at Rohini, to all the questions he was asking, "How many suitcases do you have? Do you have woollens or warm clothes?" Actually, that is what clinched the matter. Guddi had a sweater and a shawl. The man said he would lend her an overcoat till she met her relative since it was very cold outside. Then Guddi began to follow him. As Rohini watched the receding figure, she had mixed feelings. "Do you think that guy is okay?" she asked the airhostess.

"We will anyway inform our ground crew about her," said the airhostess.

As Rohini saw Guddi getting off, she realised she would never know what happened to her. Did her stupid husband take her home? Was he married to someone else? Was he alive? She had asked Guddi for her address in London, but Guddi had refused to tell her. In fact, though she had confided so much, she remained secretive. Once again, as Rohini, had often understood, you cannot help anyone. If they wish for help, then they will change their whole lives. Anyway, she gave her Anju's number. Anju, her classmate from school, was a UK citizen. She was not sure if Anju would help or if Guddi would contact her, but for what it was worth, she kept it....

Rohini just prayed for her and wished Guddi's husband would not turn out to be a bad guy after all. After four hours, the flight took off for the next lap of 10 hours.

For most part of the remaining flight, Rohini slept. Guddi had tired her. Maybe Guddi can become a writer, mused Rohini, as she recollected a conversation with a friend of hers who also loved to write. She had said, "Rohini, I have been closely studying every writer and I find they have very interesting lives, Adventurous lives. They either run away from home, live in a slum, smoke pot or leave their husband to live with another man, have different gender preferences for partners...you know they were not boring people like us. You and I are too conventional...what can we write between breakfast and lunch, except mention detergents and vegetables to buy. We will never be able to make it as writers."

Rohini too had felt like that. She could write about schools, housekeeping and television shows or the Mall. But you never know, stories could pop out of nowhere. She could check out if America was still a land of opportunities… Rohini thought, as she pulled her blanket closer.

Even before she landed in America, the news channels and newspaper headlines in India were screaming, "Bomb blast in London's northern train station…Indian suicide bomber identified as Guddi along with…."

Custom-Made

I was introduced to her as Padma Patti. However, Padma Patti saw me as a waste of time. Not yet seven years old, I was not ready for marriage, so I did not interest her. Then there was my mother who wanted me to study rather than being married off, which was something Padma Patti had never heard of. She had got married when she was only eight years of age. In her time, that was the age when most girls were married off. My mother had got married when she was 12 years of age. Which was late, according to Padma Patti, who was my father's mother's aunt. So, she styled herself as my mother's mother-in-law, though she was just a few years older than her. Padma Patti was younger than my father.

However, except for the fact that she wanted me to get married when I was eight years old, Padma Patti had a calm demeanour and an air of knowing all that needed to be known, particularly regarding matters concerning women. She knew what was right and wrong and how a woman's life should be. She did not question any injustice to women because she never saw them as unfair practices. She was very humble and receptive to whatever a male member of the family said, even if it was my brother who was still in his teens. His words carried more weight that my sister's or even my mother's.

Padma Patti did not live with us but she visited us fairly frequently. We lived in Kumbakonam, the temple city, and she always came on a pilgrimage. She came alone and brought a cloth bag which carried her second sari. For the rest, there was a stove and a set of vessels in our house that were used only when she came. I don't know if they belonged to her or not, but she was the only one who used them, and she did so with a sense of ownership. The stove was a cast iron coal-fired one, was called a *kumuti adupu*.

She was alone as she had no sibling. Though married so early, girls would not be sent to the in-law's house till they attained puberty. Padma Patti too got married, but continued to live in her parent's house. The only difference was that she now wore a gold *mangalsutra* around her neck, toe rings, a nose pin and diamond earrings. She wore flowers on her hair and had her bath with a profusion of turmeric, so much so that her skin had a yellow hue. She was a beautiful young girl with bright eyes and full lips, with long thick hair which was the pride of her parents and her in-laws too. By nature, she was chirpy and ready with a smile.

One day, the young lad of 14 or 15 years who was her husband, had gone to the fields to help his father who was a farmer. That was what he did every day, going with his father to cultivate crops. But that day turned out to be different. A snake bit him and before his father could rush to his son, before the local medicine-man could suck out the venom, the young boy succumbed to the rising poison in his body. A message was soon sent to Padma Patti's family to inform them that she had lost her husband. She was a widow.

Padma Patti did not understand much of what had happened. She definitely did not grieve as she hardly knew this fellow they called her husband. When her jewellery was taken off, Padma did not like it. Slowly, more and more restrictions were placed on her. Then Padma realised it was not nice to be a widow. That meant she would never have a home, children or a family. She would have to live in the backyard of someone's house so that she was seen as little as possible. She represented bad luck and it was considered a bad omen if she was seen anywhere. All these realisations came to her bit by bit. As a 10-11 year old all the ramifications of widowhood were not understood by her. And yet she slipped into her new role with ease. "All this must be true," she thought. "My bad karma."

Mangalam lived on the same street, in the backyard of her parents' house. She was 14 years of age. She was also a widow. She had gone to live in her husband's home but soon after, her husband fell ill with typhoid and passed away. Mangalam came back to her house within a year. Another young widow, Vanaja, was much older than both of them. She had a son who was being brought up by her brother-in-law and his wife. Vanaja also stayed with them and did a major share of the household chores. These three girls and a few others became friends. That is why Mangalam Patti also used to come with Padma Patti to Kumbakonam, once in a while.

Both Padma and Mangalam were widowed in their pre-puberty years. No function was performed for them when they attained puberty as was done for all other girls. They were not allowed to wear flowers in their hair and generally wore hand-me-down saris. They were not allowed to go out of the house during the day lest anyone catch sight of them. They had to bathe in the river early in the morning before sunrise, when the likelihood of anyone else being awake and on the road, was minimal. And for the rest of the day, they could not step out. They performed chores for the person in whose house they lived. Only after a certain age would their heads be tonsured. Once that was done, they were allowed to roam about freely. But till then they were house-bound.

Padma seemed to accept her new conditions. Mangalam came knocking on her door and before anyone was up, they both would giggle and run down to the river for a bath. There used to be a pious and respected Brahmin of the village called Ananthachari, who lived in the house opposite Padma Patti's. Both Mangalam and Padma felt they spotted him lurking in the shadows of dawn when they were bathing. One week, Mangalam was down with fever and Padma had to go alone. It was then that she was sure she saw Ananthachari. He even beckoned to her from behind the thicket. Padma was repulsed by him and scared. She ran back home. The next day she went to bathe a little late so that there would be more light. It would be easier to avoid Ananthachari then. But he was somehow always around when she went to the river. Three days a month she did not have to bathe and was the happiest then. If it was not for Mangalam, she would not have been able to bathe what with Ananthachari peeping at them all the time. Ananthachari was wary when the two of them were together. One day, after it was no longer a suspicion but a confirmed truth that it was Ananthachari who was making advances to her in the darkness of dawn, he came to her parent's house. He shielded his eyes with a towel, keeping a small aperture open. Knocking on the door, he told her father, "No, no, I am not coming in, not when that ill-fated daughter of yours is walking about. Tell her not to go to bathe at sunrise because she comes before my eyes first thing in the morning! *Ayyo*, what to say of my fate! I have to see her when I come out for my *sandhyavandana…ayyo, karmam karmam." Sandhyavandana* is the prayer performed at twilight, three times a day. Ruing his bad karmas he had exclaimed, *Ayyo karmam, karmam.*

Padma's father was irritated that his inauspicious daughter would bathe after sunrise. "Tell her to behave herself," rasped her father to her mother. Her mother too said, "Be like Vanaja…." The next few years were tough till her head was tonsured and she was made to wear a *narmadi.* This was a sari, silkish in texture and light brown in colour.

I heard that my father had tried again to stop this practice…his first attempt had been with his mother. He had failed. So he stood even less chance to influence Padma's Patti's parents, but he is said to have tried his best. With my paternal grandmother, the story went like this. My grandfather passed away and my grandmother wanted to shave her head. My father would not hear of it. She was staying with us and one day we all had gone to a temple. While in the sanctum sanctorum, the priest would place what is called a *shadari* on the head of each devotee waiting for *darshan* or offering prayers to a deity. It is like wearing God's crown for a few split seconds. It is placed only on a woman's head if her husband husband is alive (a man could be a widower, no problems). But since my grandmother had not shaved off her hair, the priest did not know she was a widow and placed the *shadari* on her head. This made my grandmother very uncomfortable because she felt she had sinned before God.

The next morning, she quietly called a barber and got her hair shaved off. No one knew. When my father saw her, he was livid, but what could be done?

Other than my father, a distant relative, there was no one to protest against Padma's tonsure. Her own parents got her to wear the *narmadi* also. Very few widows could afford a *narmadi* and instead, wore plain white cotton saris. Padma's parents were considered to have made a sacrifice for spending so much even on their widowed daughter. Once her head was tonsured and she wore a *narmadi*, she could walk around freely. People like Ananthachari still bothered her though. Even when on pilgrimages, lecherous men stared at her. But as time went on, Padma could not care less. She accepted that as their nature. She went to so many temples and particularly loved the Ramaswamy temple in Kumbakonam and that is why she often came to our house.

She followed a routine wherever she went. She would rise early, collect firewood, light the stove and place a *vengala panai* (a pot made of five metals) with rice to cook it. The vessel would be smeared with rice flour so it did not catch much soot, therefore making it easier to wash. She would cook a meal, eat herself and leave the rest for the family with whom she was staying, in this case, us. My mother would not be allowed to cook. Padma Patti would use a lot of tamarind in her food, I remember and I had to eat only that.

In our house, when Padma Patti was not visiting, the routine was slightly different. My mother and father would have their morning coffee soon after waking up. When my mother mixed the decoction with milk, she took it to my father. When Padma Patti was with us, she would be watching. Though she understood the many ways of widowhood, she never could appreciate the ways of married women. For one, she never learnt that the husband was referred to with respect. When she spoke of her husband whom she had met only once, she used to use an informal address. She also could not understand why people had coffee in the morning. She would have her bath, cook and eat, with nothing to drink in the morning. So, before my mother came back after giving my father his coffee, she would add a lot of hot water into my mother's decoction. My mother never got strong coffee which she loved. This was Padma Patti's way of expressing her disapproval of the coffee drinking habit.

My father would teach my mother English for half an hour before he left for college, where he taught English. Padma Patti, like many others today, could not understand why my mother had to learn at all and that too, the English language. It would not help her be a better wife. Padma Patti was not jealous or bitter, but was just like any other woman who believed wives should not study, could not flirt with their husbands, should not make any special food for themselves and so on. She and people like her would gossip, argue and lay down rules, but never curse their fate. They did not even protest at the way society was treating them.

Padma Patti felt she was born to live the way she did.

One day, when she was in our home, my father's elder brother visited us. He had lost his wife many, many years ago and they did not have any children. He, unlike men of those times, did not remarry. Padma Patti saw him as an ethical man, pious, appreciative of her cooking and soft-spoken. "*Eka patni vratam* (vow to have only one wife)," she remarked softly and admiringly. My uncle, too, paused in his thoughts. His heart was torn apart as he reflected on the injustice done to those experiencing widowhood. But that was all that could happen.

I Did My Mother Proud

"I could even kill myself to earn enough for my family," I said in desperation to my colleague and friend, Abhishek Nath. Abhishek nodded. I knew he also felt this. We both were having tea and bread *pakora*s in the NGO, STC (Save The Children) canteen. This canteen was better in the sense that it was less crowded than our office one. In the office canteen you never knew who was eavesdropping on you. So, Abhishek and I preferred to come here for our evening tea. During the day we never got out of our seats and even worked through lunch. Abhishek was in the despatch section and I was looking after the photo section. We both worked in the Jawan Samachar division of the government's Defence Ministry.

Abhishek had two children, while I have four. Perhaps that is why I used such strong language and he simply nodded. Abhishek's wife had recently got a job as a secretary in a private firm so that was also another reason why he perhaps felt less desperate.

My life is another story. My mother at the age of 80 is still energetic and interested in goings-on and cannot understand the concept of a limited income. Her other sons, my two brothers, live abroad in Canada and send her dollars every now and then. She pretends to understand when I tell her I do not earn enough, but cannot help ending each conversation with: "Son, then why don't you give it all up and go join your brothers?"

She felt the only way to save me from damnation was to make constant demands on me so that one day I would also go to Canada and earn in lakhs. "You have two daughters. How will you get them married if you carry that stupid brown briefcase and go to your office on your scooter, day in and day out?" she would ask. She would also express her disgust at my job to all our neighbours, in our family circle, shopkeepers, just everybody. She would say, "And if his father had not left him this house, this boy would perhaps be on the road with his four children."

A loud mother or mother-in-law generally affects her daughters-in-law by making them meek, I think. My wife is a very quiet person. Slim even after four children, she is very subtle and gentle. She has never once told me she had low blood pressure. She definitely needs much more nutrition. At the back of my mind, I feel that she does not eat enough because she wants to keep food aside for the children. Not that we are poor, but we measure the delicacies we buy or make. She was also so timid that she would not listen to my suggestion of taking up a job. As it happened, the only time I managed to convince her to join a nursery school as a teacher, one of the school children got meningitis and died. It upset her so much that she felt if she had only taken a little more care and told the child's parents that she suspected meningitis, she could have helped to save the child. The logic was skewed, but the fact was that it upset her and instead of going to school in the days that followed, she spent most of her time with the child's mother. And that was the end of my dream of getting a few hundred rupees extra every month.

Abhishek was saying it was getting late, so we trudged back to the fourth floor where our office was. As I slipped back behind my desk and on to my chair, I began my favourite pastime again—how to make more money. I taught math as tuition to Class X children after office. I had only two students and wondered how I could increase that number. Even before that I went on to add up how much I would earn with six students and how I would require at least 10 to give me adequate money, I could see the faces of my children and my beaming mother….

That evening when I went to the parking lot, a tall man came up to me and introduced himself as Kamal. He started a polite conversation, then asked me if I could give him a ride on my scooter. He seemed to know where I was going, but it never occurred to me to ask him how he knew this. Later, I found out that he worked in the travel agency in the building next to mine. He stayed further away from my house, about three miles ahead. From that day onwards he rode with me to and from office and after a few days even wanted to share the cost of petrol. I refused. He was not making me go out of my way and I was traversing this route anyway. Soon we started stopping at Panchi Chaiwallah for a cup of tea before going home. Kamal felt since he was not paying for the petrol, he could at least treat me. I enjoyed this because I had to go straight to my student's house and the tea made me feel more energetic.

One day, Kamal introduced me to a friend of his. Kamal always tried to help me think of new ways to earn. Last week, he helped me to bargain and sell my old scooter because he had another friend who sold me a brand new scooter because he felt too scared to drive it. Since he wanted to get rid of it, I got it for a throwaway price. Even my wife valued Kamal's niceness. Then another friend of Kamal invested Rs 50 of mine to make it Rs 1000 in just six months. I suddenly got a new life and felt that this improvement may make my mother proud of me before she died!

Kamal's new friend was sober and quiet. He told me about all the job vacancies he knew of and the many contacts he had. But I did not want to quit my job. In another two months I could retire and get a pension. The pressure on me was mounting because my elder daughter had got a good proposal from the parents of a boy who had a Master's in Business Administration (MBA) degree from none other than the Indian Institute of Management (IIM) in Ahmedabad. Abhishek in fact, had choked with surprise when I told him this. I needed money for her marriage. I may have been able to manage the amount that the wedding would cost me if it had not been for the fact that my elder son had got admission in Stanford for a Master's in engineering. They promised him funding from the second semester, but I had to pay for the first. My second daughter had got admission in the course in architecture, but the fee was so exorbitant that she never told me this. She said she would join a Regional Engineering college because she knew I would not be able to pay. She was also selected to dance in the International Dance Festival to be held in Paris in November, three months from now. She needed costumes to be stitched.

Would you believe it when I told you that the youngest, so careless and fun-loving, had started working hard at improving his tennis? Every day his coach met me on my morning walk and persuaded me to fund him. Tennis is an expensive game and I had tried to veer him towards cricket long, long ago. But my wife's brother had come for a short stay once and he bought him his first racquet. Ever since he had been sending him pocket money to keep his tennis up. Since he had reached the national level, a greater investment was needed. His coach also wanted to send him to various tournaments, but these were not necessarily funded by the stadium. That is why I planned all day on how to make money!

But that is only the simpler part of the story. Five years ago, I had taken a loan. My mother had nagged me about the house crumbling down and the lack of maintenance on my part. It was then that I bought my scooter too. Abhishek had suggested it. "How long will your mother live?" he had asked. "Take a loan against the house and after your mother passes away, sell it. You will not only be able to repay the loan but also meet the children's requirements and save for your old age. A house is a dead investment."

Nothing sounded truer. That loan helped me send my daughter to Singapore, Malaysia, Indonesia and other countries along with her dance teacher on a performance tour. Also, I was able to get my elder son excellent tuitions and that dear boy had been so grateful that he had worked very hard to get one distinction after another. My wife had wisely taken a little from me and started building a saving at a jewellery store and even purchased a chain and bangles for our daughter.

The twist in the story is that my mother was healthy, God bless her, but I could not sell my house. The interest had mounted and now to repay that loan was my nightmare. If I had to meet all my financial commitments, I needed about Rs 25 lakhs and only my house would get me about 15 or so. What would I still do about the remaining amount? Sometimes I thought I would go mad.

Kamal's friend, LNJ, was now my best friend. He would sit for hours and add energy to my dreams with possible solutions. The money he made for me with future trading became less, as the market was low. I never understood how he was making money and so when he told me he could not do it any longer, I just accepted the reality.

One evening, the bank manager dropped in at home. Luckily, my mother had not met him or else she would have interrogated him and found out that I had takena loan with my house as the mortgage. My wife never suspects me and so did not feel the need to ask him why he had come. She told him I was not at home and offered him tea or coffee. Since nobody feels like hurting my wife, the manager had politely refused, complimented her on the house and asked for a number to get in touch with me. She gave my student's phone number saying I would be taking tuitions now. Sure enough, he called me there but thankfully not from my house. He used really foul language! He also threatened to issue a warrant for my arrest if I did not begin paying up.

That evening, before finishing with my tuitions, I called LNJ and told him I would like to meet him. We met at Panchi Chaiwallah. He heard me out and offered to take me a man who was not only influential but also had many spiritual powers. "He has such influence that if he says one word, they will waive all your loans," LNJ told me.

Ever since that evening I have been regularly paying my respects to that man whom I have begun to call my mentor. He taught me some prayers and told me that a solution would be found. A week later, he gave me Rs 10,000 and told me to pay it as my first instalment. "Do not ask where it came from," he said. "God helps the needy."

That gave me a lot of relief and it was then that I told my wife, Suchitra about him. She is old-fashioned and wanted to know what religion he followed, whether he was a Tantric, a charismatic Christian and so on. I told her I knew the answers to none of those questions, but would definitely take her one day to meet him. When I told him that I wanted to bring my wife, he said he did not meet women. I had also observed that there were no women in his meetings. Anyway, my wife could never meet him, but she kept nurturing her ideas that he was a Tantric and was trying to hypnotise me or he was a fundamentalist who did not hesitate to kill. In this way, she went on warning me all the time.

Sometimes I too felt a sudden stab of fear. If this mentor of mine asked for the Rs 10,000 he had given me, where would I go? Was I getting into more trouble? As though sensing my discomfort, he got me two new students for tuitions. It became my daily routine to go to the ashram every day after tuitions and sit outside his room till he called me. He said I was special and that God was guiding me by bringing me to him in times of trouble. I asked him for a *mantra* and which God I should pray to. He just smiled. "God is within you," he said.

After about two months, he went on his travels. Before going, he gave me another Rs 20,000 and said it was all mine. I was overwhelmed. I fell at his feet in gratitude. Inside my system, however, I felt great unease. Was it the power of the divine or was it black money? Was I falling into some trap? Anyway, to cut a long story short, it eased my immediate state, but within two weeks I was desperate again.

My wife resented my going to him. Somehow, I began to feel I had got myself into a no-win situation. My children had no hope from me, they felt I would not be able to give much. My mother had given me up long ago, but now my wife was getting irritated. I had lost touch with Abhishek on purpose because he tried to counsel me, saying I was biting more than I could chew and so on. His wife was earning in thousands, you see, and so he did not know what it was to be desperate. I told my wife that she had no right to say anything for I was making ends meet for the entire family and I, therefore, should be allowed to invest time in doing so.

While I was in this mood, LNJ came up with new suggestions. He told me to opt for voluntary retirement. Then I would get my provident fund, a gratuity and a pension. He said he would take me to teach a course, which would pay me Rs 50 lakhs per annum, if not more. "If you have the patriotic spirit," he said. I was sure that I did. I never asked them then what they understood by patriotism though.

All that happened thereafter was a whirl.

I retired. Went with LNJ to a farm where there were many people attending lectures on religions. I was beginning to feel caged when one day, LNJ and two other men called me to a room and asked me what I was living for. It was strange, but I felt they had my interest at heart when they asked me that question. I told them my commitments. I wanted a worry-free life and my mother to feel I was doing as well as my brothers. They nodded as though they understood exactly what I meant. They took care of me thereafter.

I paid all my loans. I renovated the house and gave my children all they wanted. Only my wife said I had betrayed her. But I told her she had brought it on us. If she had also taken up a job like Abhishek's wife, maybe we would not have had to take drastic measures. She had no idea about what I do. She just feels I am doing something wrong when unexplained money comes in,. She does not know what I put in to earn this. How can I explain to her? She would think I was working for some terrorist outfit. Sometimes I also feel uncomfortable but now I cannot wriggle out of anything. They have spent too much on me and I have to follow orders. If I do not…

So when my wife left to live with our youngest son in California, I did not protest. She may be safer there I thought. Of course she was not divorcing me or leaving me or anything like that. "Your mother looks after you," she said, which was true. My mother looks after me as she never has before. She does not worry about whether the money is earned through right means or not. She has to be better off than her neighbours and family, which I have now been able to do for her. At 96, she is still going strong. All the children are away.

Sometimes I miss my family...I do not know whether my actions are wrong. But then they would all have said I was a useless father. At least now people think highly of me... except for my wife, that is... and my children are successful and want me to go to them...they don't know what I do, so they get irritated when I say I cannot tell them. But here they will not let me go. When I miss my family, however, a kind of fear keeps crawling inside me. We all live with one kind of fear or other...is mine crippling? Well, I am also sacrificing my life for the nation, for a cause and that too incognito. Think of that. My job is built on the idea of hatred and killing. I cannot tell you more.

We are planning an event in another three months. Till now I have been lucky. Knowing my trait of obedience, the higher-ups always kept me to run errands and doing back-office work. Of course, even on a simple errand, I am always ready to detonate the bomb in my pocket, if I get caught... that is an essential part of the training.

But now my mother does not say I am her useless son. She is proud of me.

Josiyar Ayya

Srinivasa Iyengar crossed the street. He lived just opposite the Munsif Court (district court that handles small civic disputes) in Gobichettipalayam. Even as he was crossing the wide road, he began loosening his neckband. He was wearing a *panchakacham,* the traditional attire of brahmin men in south India; a *dhoti* tucked five times at the waist and taken between the legs too. Srinivasa Iyengar's *dhoti* was an expensive one, it had a broad gold border. He wore a sparkling white shirt with it, a black advocate's gown and the lawyer's neckband. Now the neckband was in his gown's pocket. Though the sun was shining happily and the temperature was high, there was a pleasant breeze . His peon Chellapa was walking behind him, carrying the umbrella over his head. It was a trifle challenging because Srinivasa Iyengar was about 5 feet 11 inches tall, while Chellapa was all of 5 feet. So he stood on tiptoes and stretched his hand way up as he held the tip of the umbrella so that his master was well shielded from the sunrays.

Today had been a good day at court. Srinivasa Iyengar had just won the case for his client…just as his astrologer had predicted. He had charged a hefty fee and the client had been more than happy to pay it, considering that he (the client) had a huge foundry in Coimbatore and so could afford it. Srinivasa Iyengar could not hide his joy. It was a hat-trick. Yesterday, that is Thursday and on the bygone Tuesday, he had won two cases. Though his fee had not been so handsome in those two cases, he had still earned enough for the whole month.

Srinivasa Iyengar was happy because though he was trained to be a lawyer, his true passion lay elsewhere. He loved to act and was one of the founding members of the drama company in his town. He also loved to solve crossword puzzles. The newspapers carried a crossword every day and the correct answer to the puzzle would be rewarded with what was a handsome sum of money—Rs 10. He responded to every crossword puzzle he came across. Fortunately, he did not have a mathematical bent of mind, which meant that he never added up all that he spent as fees to enter the competition and the postage charges incurred. He just felt disappointed when he did not win. He did not feel any monetary loss when he sent in entries after entries to one single crossword, hoping one of them would be the completely right one, the prize-winning one. Over the past 15 years, he had won Rs 2 once and held on to that memory with great pride.

As he entered the gate to his house, his three sisters who had come visiting were chatting in the verandah. Since they were all elder to him, they pampered him. Srinivasa Iyengar smiled generously at them and nodded his head in assent when he was asked if he was ready for lunch. He quickly climbed up the stairs and as he did so, was pulling his shirt over his head. His shirt had only three buttons below the collar. These three buttons were ornate diamond buttons, strung together in a chain that he fixed into the buttonholes of any shirt he wore. The shirt itself was worn over the head.

Then he untied his belt. A green belt with leather pockets and a zip. One leather pocket was for his glasses, the other one contained change, while the zip was for the notes and his court card. He gently unzipped this section and took out Rs 100 which he placed inside his cupboard safely, under the neatly stacked white *dhoti*s. He wound the sacred thread falling across his bare shoulder over his ear as he went into the backyard of the house, which is where the toilet was located. A few minutes later he came into the dining room with his hands and feet washed and cleaned, his sacred thread back to running across his chest and a towel thrown over his shoulders, almost covering his chest. He sat down to a hot meal, but before that called out to Chellapa, "Chellapa go call Josiyar Ayya. Tell him I am at home."Josiyar Ayya meant the astrologer. Chellapa who was outside the window, answered in the affirmative and ran to do his bidding.

Josiyar Ayya whose name was Vedantam, was another of Srinivasa Iyengar's weaknesses. Srinivasa Iyengar himself was a good astrologer but liked to discuss horoscopes with Vedantam, particularly his own. It was Vedantam who had predicted 10 years ago that his wife was likely to fall ill. He said it gently and Srinivasa Iyengar had not taken it seriously. But lo and behold! Within two years of his prediction, she did fall ill and even passed away, leaving behind a little daughter.

After that Srinivasa Iyengar paid great heed to whatever Vedantam said. Last month he had told him that there would be a substantial increase in his earned income and was that not coming true? To Srinivasa Iyengar it was a great surprise because being a civil lawyer, he rarely got cases. When he did, the payment was not handsome enough. His colleague Ramakrishna Iyer was a criminal lawyer. He earned so much, as they said, he had both hands full. But Srinivasa Iyengar was not envious. His kind of practice gave him enough time to pursue his interests and yet feed his family.

Srinivasa Iyengar had married again. His wife was 15 years younger than him. A pretty woman, she could sing beautifully, cooked extremely well and even knew a little bit of astrology. His first wife had been soft-spoken, less aware of the world and more docile. Kamala, his present wife, was a woman in her own right and Srinivasan felt somehow curbed in his style with her. She found him silly to waste money on crossword puzzles, found it juvenile that he should rehearse for his plays when he could be working on a case and so on. They both saw eye to eye when they heard music or discussed astrology. That was also the reason why Vedantam had a special place in their house. Kamala was at that moment in her father's house in Musiri, a town which lay on the other side of the Kaveri River. She was expecting their first child.

Within half an hour, Vedantam arrived and while Srinivasa Iyengar sat on the swing in the hall, Vedantam sometimes sat with him there, but sometimes in a huge comfortable cane chair. There was a table in front of the swing which had many horoscopes lying on it along with plain paper and pencils. That day they both sat on the swing with the horoscopes between them. Neatly handwritten in a leather-bound notebook, the four corners and centre were marked with turmeric and the centre also had a red spot on the yellow turmeric.

They were served hot coffee. Vedantam was happy Srinivasa Iyengar had earned well. It meant that he too would then get a handsome *dakshina* (payment). As they poured over the movements of the planets, Saturn and Jupiter, the retrograde Rahu and Ketu, Vedantam suddenly stopped. "Enough for today, sir, I think the time is not right…let me go home," said Vedantam.

"But we have just begun…was the coffee cold? Shall I get you another cup?" said Srinivasa Iyengar.

"The omens are not right. Don't ask me more questions. Let us see some other time," said Vedantam.

"Come on, tell me what you see…you look like you have seen a *gandam*" laughed Srinivasa Iyengar. A look at Vedantam's face made him ask softly, "You have?" Gandam is said to be a challenging period in astrology and in this particular case Srinivasa Iyengar was referring to a period which could indicate death.

"These things are not said, but yes, there is a likely *gandam*…a *gandam* is just an inauspicious period. One must be careful. We can avert it too…we can perform rituals to overcome it," said Vedantam speaking forcefully as though to convince himself.

Srinivasa Iyengar knew very well that the *gandam* Vedantam was seeing in his horoscope was the *yamagandam* or the inauspicious possibility of death. The discussion now took another turn as the two serious men were discussing life and death. Neither of them had even an iota of doubt that their interpretation of the horoscope could be wrong. They drew the charts again and again, the *rasi* chart, which is the basic chart showing the positions of the nine planets at birth in the twelve zodiac signs, the more complicated *navamsa* chart which showed the ninth part of each sign and calculated the *dasa* period which showed the planet that would be ruling at different times and so on…they did not seem to find any reason why they could be wrong Of course, Srinivasa Iyengar wanted to live since he was just 30 years of age. "If you cross this *gandam*, you will live very long," Vedantam had said and these words rung in his ears all night, all morning, all the time.

Kamala was eight months pregnant. She was excited about having a child. She was all of 15 years old. She was the eldest of 10 siblings (the 11th had not arrived at this point in their lives) and her father had got her married to a widower because that was all he could afford. Though he was holding a high position as an inspector of schools, he knew that with six more daughters to get married off and his family still growing, he would have to be careful right from the start. And the person he had chosen for his daughter was a good man from a well-known family, so he did not hesitate to get his eldest daughter, the apple of his eye, married to him. Initially, Kamala had been a little disappointed and wary, but then she found he was not a bad man. He would tease her by singing *Kamala lochana*, a song composed by the great composer Thyagaraja in praise of Lord Rama. But Srinivasa Iyengar would look at

Kamala's eyes and sang the song to say her eyes were like that of a lotus petal. Kamala liked that. The only problem with him was that he preferred to play the role of Harishchandra, a king from Hindu mythology known for his commitment to truth or even Kaikeyi, the consort of the Ramayana's King Dasaratha (he could look like quite a beautiful woman!) in plays that were staged every Friday evening rather than going to the temple or trying to get more cases to fight in court. A play was staged after five evenings of rehearsals, so her husband was busy all evenings. During the day, after court hours, he would do crossword puzzles. Invariably, in the afternoons Vedantam, their family astrologer, would visit. Vedantam liked Kamala's coffee and told her he had never got such good coffee in this house earlier. Kamala liked that... the ghost of the first wife used to haunt her now and then. Therefore, Vedantam's words were reassuring.

One evening as Kamala was stringing jasmine buds in her parental home to offer to the Lord, her father came hurrying back in his *jatka vandi* (horse-driven cart). "Amma," he said looking at her, "come, we have to go, we have to go," he said disjointedly and in anguish.

"What happened, Appa?" asked Kamala.

Her father did not answer her. Waving a telegram, he went indoors calling out, "Janaki, Janaki..." and very soon Kamala knew the contents of the telegram. It said Srinivasa Iyengar had passed away. Kamala was heartbroken as was her father. Her whole family was dazed and defeated. The mother, Janaki, was also pregnant and she was almost full-term. She could not travel, but Kamala left with her father immediately for Gobichettipalayam. En route they had to pass the Kaveri

River. No boatsman was available. Fortunately, there was not much water in the Kaveri at that time of the year. And yet, the father and daughter gazed in despair at the water flowing in front of them. Kamala, whose belly was quite big by now, just hitched up her sari and walked into the waters. It came up to her knees. She was not very tall, maybe 4 feet 11 inches. Her father waded through the river behind his daughter. His anguish made him weaker than ever.

Walking in a wet sari which clung to her legs was not easy. And that too, when she was already feeling so heavy, both physically and emotionally. Having crossed the river, they hailed another *jatka vandi* and reached Srinivasa Iyengar's house. The distraught father and daughter entered to find the three sisters-in-law chatting in the verandah. "What happened? Where is he?' asked Kamala, her lips quivering and her hands trembling. Her father could not even say that much. They smiled and pointed indoors. Kamala knew they did not like her but would they be so cruel as to smile? Could they be so heartless? They even looked surprised to see her. As she went in, the swing was swaying and Srinivasa Iyengar was reclining on it singing Kamala *lochana* in Raga Bhairavi… Kamala rubbed her eyes in disbelief, her head reeled, everything seemed afloat and she could not see properly. She held on to her father's arm.

It was the father who addressed his son-in-law as "Mappilai?" Were they seeing a ghost?

Srinivasa Iyengar cleared his throat and smiled. Looking at his father-in-law, he spoke to his wife, "Vedantam told me that I was under the influence of a *gandam* and the best remedy was to make you cry for me. That was the reason why we staged a mock death. So, I sent you that telegram. Now you have given me new life," he said.

Was Kamala to be happy or angry? She told the story again and again for the next 50 years to decide what her emotion should have been. Srinivasa Iyengar just smiled every time his wife retold the story, sometimes exaggerating this and sometimes that. But he never said anything. He had tricked the planets with that one stroke and that remained his pride.

Additionally, he had lived to win one more prize of Rs 100 from crosswords in those past 50 years.

What's in a Name

The names of the prize-winners were being announced and I stood up, not to receive a prize but, to give them away. I had donated a large sum of money to the school in my mother's memory. Therefore, I had been invited by the school to be the chief guest at the annual day programme. A young teacher stood by me, handing me the certificates and prizes while another teacher was calling out the names of the students. The principal of the school was standing on the other side of me, beaming. My mother and some of her friends had been instrumental in setting up this school, many decades ago. She used to follow its progress, though she was not an active administrator. It was a residential school for girls, particularly from the economically weaker section of society.

"Be quick, Tejahprabha," said the principal. I thought she was speaking to me…rather a commanding tone to be used when addressing the chief guest, I thought, but she burst out, "Sorry, madam, that teacher is also called Tejaprabha." She was the one who was handing the certificates to me. I was a little taken aback and unhappy. Till today I had not met another person named Tejahprabha. If you googled my name, only I appeared. There were many Prabhas and many Tejaswinis and so on but not Tejahprabha. Now I would have to share my Google page with her. I wondered who had named her…I must ask her after the programme is over, I thought. I stole a quick glance at her. Petite and dusky, she reminded me of someone, but that name eluded me.

Anyway, I was not feeling very magnanimous towards her as she had stolen my name, I felt. My mother had named me. Tejahprabha was the name of a weapon the sage Vishwamitra gave Rama and Lakshmana…it was a weapon that could destroy the glory of the enemy, that is, making the enemy powerless without killing or hurting them. So my mother would say, "Be kind and loving. It's only then that your enemies will automatically be rendered powerless."

I kept thinking of my mother as I mechanically smiled and wished the children "Best of luck" when they came to collect their awards. How she had quietly but surely contributed to the well-being of the women around her. Among the many incidents that came to memory was that of Valli. Perhaps because that ended as mysteriously as it began.

We lived in Mandi House in New Delhi, the grounds of the Delhi residence of the Raja of Mandi. His palace stood in the centre, while all around it were hutments. After the privy purses were abolished, these were taken over by the government and allotted as government quarters for civil servants and journalists, who lived in those 30-odd residences. We too lived in one of them.

We had a domestic help called Rashu. Maybe his name was Raju but he was always called Rashu. He came from Salem and was alone; there was never any mention about a family…Rashu lived in our servants' quarters.

There were two Tamil-speaking domestic helps from Salem in that colony. The other was a maid named Valli. What to say of Valli? How to describe her? If I say she had a translucent figure, you will ask me if she let light pass through her ribs. No, she did not…but it seemed that she never took up any space. There was a wispy quality about her physical body, very light in her steps, in her movements and very fragile-looking…in ancient Indian texts, beautiful women were always described as slim-waisted, which Valli was. But let me begin with her face, or maybe her dusky complexion. She had thick long hair, always tied up at the nape of her neck into a bun that never came loose, given the amount of housework she did. Only one day I saw her with a long snake-like plait falling way below her hips. Her eyes were like stars, but they never spoke to you…they seemed to hold secrets. Her nose was just the right size, sharp and slightly upturned. I don't remember her lips…she was pleasantly buxom and not too tall. She wore her sari as women of Salem did, the proud possessor of a wardrobe of three or four saris, given by different ladies she worked for.

Valli worked in a few houses in our colony and in the Sikandra House hutments. That was just opposite the main road and those hutments too were government quarters. Those who lived in the Sikandra Road hutments said Valli lived in Mandi House and those who lived in Mandi house said Valli lived in the Sikandra Road hutments. No one knew where she lived, but it was not a mystery, just the tyranny of languages. Valli did not know Hindi though she had lived for the past 10 years in Delhi, or so she said. Once, she regaled us with a story of how her attempts at speaking Hindi had met with disastrous results. She had been working for a couple who were nice to her. The husband used to work in an "office" and the wife was a social worker. One day there was a programme in the husband's office in which the wife was also participating. The two of them had prepared some slogans and written them out on paper. The husband came home and told Valli, "I am taking these slogans with me. Tell Madam."

The wife called and Valli told her, "*Saab nari ko le kar chala gaya*." Slogans are called *nare* in Hindi, while *nari* means a woman!

After the fight she caused between the couple, Valli stopped speaking Hindi. She followed a simple modus operandi, "I don't try to understand. If their tone is kind I say *han* (yes). If unkind, I say *nahi* (no)."

So if people asked her, "Do you live in Mandi House?" she would reply in the affirmative. If they asked her authoritatively, "Do you live in the servants' quarters here?" she would say no. So her answers were never clear. She lived in Bengali Market, which was neither Mandi House nor Sikandra Road, but opposite both of them.

Valli used to come after her work finished in other residences, to our house.

My mother would have her afternoon coffee sitting in the lawn at the back. Rashu would also drink tea and sometimes, more often than not, Valli would join them. My mother would give her some *idli* or *upma*... as south Indian food was not easy to come by in those days. Valli would be very grateful. I think Rashu was also contented because I suspected he liked Valli. Both were was single, so they said. Sometimes in the afternoon I would see them sitting in the park and talking while they ate betel leaves. I had visions of Rashu getting married to Valli! However, my mother found the thought silly. "Not so easy," she said. I don't know why she said that, but she did. They both must have been above 30 years of age. Our neighbours would smile knowingly when Valli came towards our house, but my mother would never encourage gossip about them.

I looked forward to those afternoons because Valli brought me an orange peppermint when she came to our house. It was shaped like an orange clove, was sugary and a little tangy. My mother never bought these for me and it was only Valli who got them for me. They were the cheapest peppermints available, I later learnt.

One day, my mother commented rather out of context, "Valli seems to be putting on weight."

"Oh, don't tell me you think so. She is pregnant," said Mrs Mohindroo who stayed two houses to our left. My mother clammed up. Later she told me she too had thought so and that is why she was worried. If Valli got pregnant, people would not let her live in peace since she was a single woman. At that time, though I overheard conversations about Valli, they never made sense till I grew up.

Soon winter came along and Valli would wear a huge shawl so no one could make out if she was pregnant or just plump. My mother said she asked Rashu why Valli was not coming to drink tea these days. He seems to have told her she had not been speaking with him…was avoiding him and was not even regular in her work.

There were five houses in our quadrangle. We lived to the extreme left. Next to us were the Chopras. The third house was said to be a one-room, small house, but was always empty, just filled with some packing material and hay. Some old CPWD (Central Public Works Department) furniture would also be lying there. The Mohindroos lived in the fourth house and the Kumars in the fifth.

One winter morning, Rashu looked very upset. I do not know what he said, but my mother and he went to the locked house and tried to peer in. I heard my mother calling out to Valli, but there was no response. Too many cobwebs on the door meant that no one could see anything, even through the glass panes. Soon it got around that Valli had got into that house and locked herself in. Rashu had seen her go in and that is what he came and told my mother. Our neighbours were excited…something was happening in their otherwise boring lives of Chitrahar and Sunday movies on the television.

'She has been acting strange for the past few days," said Mrs Mohindroo.

"I am telling you she is pregnant…" said Mrs Kumar.

"Maybe she has gone in to deliver…" said another.

I heard my mother speaking through the locked doors, saying that she would look after her and could take her to the hospital but the door did not open and no response came. Rashu was very anguished. He could also feel the accusing eyes of the people around.

"Amma, it is not me," he cried to my mother. My mother believed him.

I saw them leaving some food outside the door, but found it untouched the next morning, that is, it was untouched by Valli, if she was there inside. Later, stray dogs had upturned the bowl and eaten the food. A small candle flame had been visible late in the previous night but soon it was extinguished. That there was someone in there was beyond doubt.

The next day passed in the same way… no news, doors closed but a periodic light telling us someone was there.

On the third day, Rashu came running, He shouted, "Amma, amma, the door is open, but she is not there…"

They all went to see the house. The back door was open and the place stank. Some bloodstains, I believe, were seen. My mother later told me, they had seen a freshly dug and covered patch on the lawn behind the house. Rashu had dug a little to see something like a placenta…but they did not disturb it more. Therefore, the story had a not-so-nice ending. Valli had conceived…she had locked herself in that empty house, killed her baby and buried it. After that, we never saw Valli in the neighbourhood. Valli was certified to be a woman with no morals and Rashu was labelled as an irresponsible male.

It disturbed my mother and Rashu immensely. "Society would have killed her," my mother was saying.

"Amma, I would have married her regardless of who the baby's father was," cried Rashu. A life lost, another deep anguish. But why it was more difficult for them (I was too young then to realise the import of what was happening and I was also not privy to a whole cogent story) was the conviction that Valli was too gentle and soft to do something like this. "If only she had taken me into confidence…I would not have judged her, " my mother said all the time, for many years after. "And I would have adopted her child." In my adult years, my mother and I would sometimes remember Valli and my mother would say, "Poor thing, I wonder if she is still alive…she had suffered a lot in her early years, married to a drunkard who used to beat her relentlessly, losing two sons in infancy and then her escape to Delhi…working as a maid and eeking out her livelihood…what was her life meant for?"

Years went past. Valli became a memory, recollected in rare moments like these. Rashu grew old with us and one day, left us, but with many fond memories to linger over. And then my mother…she could have lived longer, but she also went. I would have loved to tell her I donated part of her hard-earned money to the school…

The last award had been given. The children were happy, parents were beaming and the teachers were relieved when the function was over. The principal led me to her office before I had to face a long drive back home—this school was in Rohini which was a good 40 miles from where I lived. I was saying my thank yous and goodbyes when that teacher, my namesake, came in. Because she had my name I wanted to talk to her. She came towards me, a little apprehensively, a little eagerly.

"What does your name mean?" I asked her, almost accusingly, rather aggressively. She told me.

"A very rare name you know…it's my name too…"

"I know, madam, I was waiting to meet you. That is why I came in here. My mother named me because she kept thinking of you," said Tejahprabha Valli, as her full name read.

A Thought in Pink

"Kishaaaan…" called his mother. Kishan tried to shut out the sound by pulling his quilt over his ears, and covering his face. But the noises grew louder and became a cacophony. He could hear vessels clanging in the kitchen. The maid was at work. Every day, she had so much to tell his mother…about that husband who came home drunk and beat her again like every night, about the cold and her leaking hut and the fight between the lady in the neighbouring flat and her husband. Some pressure cookers were hissing and letting out steam in the flats around. The regular vendor pitched in too, "*Subjiwalla…alloo lo, bengan lo…*" selling vegetables beginning with what was almost a staple in Delhi, the potato. The fellow who bought old newspapers, empty beer bottles and what have you, had a distinct call, "*Kabariwallah… kabaaaadi…*," he yelled, making his way down the street. Morning had drawn apart its curtains, and the players were taking their positions…

A roaring engine smothered other sounds, the milk van and a puppy yelping. No matter what Kishan did, these sounds went through his soft quilt and kept telling him to wake up. The noises were not new to Kishan. He felt all was well with the world when he heard them. It was his habit to turn in bed, call Gaurav and discuss the plans for the day and then yell out to his mother for his morning tea, saying, "*Chai*...Mummy, *chai.*"

But today, Kishan's mother was rudely whisking the quilt off him. She had become more aggressive since his father had died. In those days, his father used to be harsh, but his mother would always protect him. Now she perhaps felt the need to play both roles, thought Kishan. "Get up...get up... it is already quarter past eight. You have to be in office by nine and you are still in bed? Do you not remember what a stickler for punctuality your father was? How to make you understand? When will you give up your childish ways?"

Kishan had grown deaf to his mother's reprimands. They were one of those "feel good" noises. Kishan went through his morning ablutions and dressed up in his light blue shirt and dark blue trousers...a security guard's uniform. With his identity card chain around his neck, his belt in place, he went to the dining room to find his mother waiting to serve his breakfast. Picking up his lunch box, he told her it was too late to eat and dashed out. His mother followed with the plate in hand and thrust mouthfuls of parathas into his mouth. Actually, Kishan liked it that way...he did not have to wash his hand sand the smell of food did not stick to his uniform. Kishan knew Guptaji would be waiting at the corner of their street. Every day he would pretend he was on his way to the bus stop and when he saw Kishan, he would ask him for a lift on his motorbike. He always asked the same questions, "Which way are you going? Near Khan Market? Oh! Thank you. Can I bother you for a lift, child?" he would say with the newness of a fresh idea every day.

All this was, however, not of primary interest to Kishan. When he turned his motorbike at one angle he could get a glimpse of the red house in the back lane. There, hearing his motorbike, the bathroom window would open and Rashmi would wave or smile, depending on the kind of audience they had. If she was not there, Kishan would give a missed call and Rashmi would fling the window open within seconds. What a fantastic moment that was!

Ever since Kishan had started working, he had not been able to meet Rashmi often enough. She was doing a course to become an air hostess. Kishan would wait for her outside her polytechnic. Sometimes Rashmi would bunk classes and they would go for a movie. But when it was time to go home, they would do so separately. No one in their colony knew as yet that Kishan and Rashmi wanted to get married. Not even their parents.

Kishan reached office on time. "Kishan *beta*, how are you? Mummy okay?" asked Uncle Dev. Dev had been his father's closest friend. "Yes, Chacha," answered Kishan as he signed the attendance register, filled up the time of entry and went upstairs to the third floor where he carried out his duties. No one could enter the third floor without showing him his identity card.

"He is such a good boy. He's the only son so a little spoilt. I got him this job," said Dev to Ram Swaroop, the new office superintendent.

"What does his father do?" asked Ram Swaroop.

"Oh, sir! I should have told you that first," said Dev, who was the oldest among the security personnel in the building. They said he knew everything, the top secrets as well as the ones top bosses never got to know.

"Kishan's father, Hari Das, was my senior. He brought me from the village and I joined about a year after him. Hariji was like my elder brother. In fact, I used to call him that. We are from the same village. My *bhabhi* or sister-in-law, Hariji's wife, is a goddess. Real *devi*. How she looked after my wife and me till we could afford accommodation!" he said, shaking his head in emotion.

"But sir, Hari *bhaiya* died last year when there was a mishap during the construction work in our office, when the new wing was being built. He was very conscientious and would not leave the office premises until everyone had left. Not a single security lapse during his period, sir, not a single lapse.

"One day he was standing on the site waiting for the last person to leave when suddenly a log of wood got loose from the scaffolding and fell right on his head. He died on the spot. It is true that Yama comes searching for you wherever you are…it was Yama, the god of death, who dropped that log on his head. I was very upset. So was my wife. But anyway, to come back to what I was telling you, I then requested that his son Kishan be appointed in his place. The director heeded my request and so here he is."

Ram Swaroop got up to go. Ever since he had been transferred to this office, he made it a point to spend some time with Dev to try and glean some secrets. Security was of great importance in the Intelligence Bureau and Ram Swaroop did not even trust the oldest hand. The onus was on him ultimately and he never forgot the first lines he had heard in his training, "Never trust anybody, not even your father." Even if he did not take that literally, Ram Swaroop followed these words very closely.

He saw Kishan on duty on the third floor. "Reduce your tummy, young man," he said, punching Kishan on his generous stomach. The parathas in Kishan's stomach squeaked under the pressure.

"What are the important lessons you have learnt? For how many days have you been coming to office?" asked Ram Swaroop.

"Two and a half months, sir," replied Kishan. "No one can pass through this gate without getting their identity card checked…and my duty is to do that. I have to check the name on the card and the tag as well as match the person's face."

"What else do you?"

"If I see anything lying around, even if it is a wrapper for a snack, I must return it to the office," said Kishan. Those were the exact words Dev Chacha had used. "Do not keep anything in your hand," Dev had said.

"Good. What else?" asked Ram Swaroop. Somehow, he did not like this young boy. His gait was not impressive and he had no energy. But he was giving the right answers.

"Sir, we should be the first to arrive and the last to leave."

"Okay, what else?"

Kishan fumbled. There did not seem anything else.

"You need more training. Meet me on Wednesday, that is, the day after tomorrow morning at nine in my office," said Ram Swaroop as he walked away, his shoes thudding on the polished floor. He would straighten out this boy. All he needed was lots of exercise and a little bit of knocking around. He would first discuss his plans with Dev on the next day.

Kishan did not like the order. Trainings were torturous and took place in the police camps where everyone always targeted his belly. They made him work more because of that! And even called him names. He would talk to Dev Chacha and wriggle out of it, he thought.

That evening as he was locking up, Kishan noticed an attractive pen drive on Mr Meena's table. He picked it up mechanically, thinking he would hand it over to Dev Chacha. But when he touched it, it was smooth and pink...like Rashmi's cheeks in winter. Kishan stood still, looking at it for some time. Then he was afraid someone may come along and ask him why he was spending so much time in the room, so he went to the next, locking one room after another, with his mind however only on the pen drive. Somehow, Kishan felt it would have been used to copy some of those sexy films...Gaurav and he loved watching them, which is why the pen drive excited him. After all, Dev Chacha would not say anything even if he found out tomorrow. He would state harmlessly, "Don't do it again, *beta*."

"Gaurav," Kishan said, calling his friend on his cell phone. "I have some *masala*, fun, for us this evening." They decided to meet in the park behind Mehrauli, where no one would disturb them. Gaurav placed his laptop on the table to charge and then bought some beer. In fact, till about three months ago this had been their routine. Both Gaurav and Kishan had finished their so-called graduation three years ago. Kishan's father had tried his best to get his son a job but Kishan found a new excuse each time to avoid this. He would take the motorbike his indulgent father had bought him when he had been in his second year of college and meet Gaurav. The two of them would stand outside either Mata Sundari girls' college or one of the many other girls' colleges by noon when classes would be getting over. They enjoyed just sitting on the motorbike, chatting and laughing having an occasional snack such as *bhel puri* or *kulcha-naan*.

In the afternoons, they would watch a movie either in the theatre or on Gaurav's laptop. Gaurav had been lucky because a foreigner had left his laptop in a taxi on his way to the airport. But there is a little background to this.

Another love Gaurav and Kishan shared was their fascination for cars. Uncle Bishen had a garage near Gaurav's house, where they would go at least three times a week. Uncle Bishen would give them tea and *samosa*s and let them help him or the mechanics there. They had learnt quite a bit about cars just by working there. Uncle Bishen also ran a taxi service. Gaurav and Kishan would drive his taxi whenever required and he would pay them for it. That served them as pocket money to buy petrol for the motorbike and other such expenses.

Once Uncle Bishen told Gaurav to pick up a gentleman from Hotel Imperial and drop him at the airport. When he came back after dropping him, Gaurav had found the laptop bag in the back seat. That is when Gaurav and Kishan actually started watching such films because that laptop itself had some recorded.

Even though they tried all the three files in the pen drive, none had any movie. One opened to show a Table, the other had only text and the third never opened. They were so disappointed. Gaurav shouted at Kishan, saying, “At least I would have brought a movie we could have seen.” They deleted the three files and Kishan put back the pink pen drive in his pocket.

Then it struck him that usually a person who entered the office was frisked. He wondered how to avoid that. He decided to put the pen drive in between his parathas and take it into the office to put it back on the same desk.

However, the night had been very troubled for Mr Meena. He suddenly remembered he had left the pen drive on his table and had forgotten to put it in the steel almirah. Meena sat with his head in his hands. His boss had asked him for a pen drive so he had given him the pink one. He had copied something from his desktop and said, “Keep this carefully. I have to take action on it tomorrow.”

Meena was used to such things and thought he would lock it up in the steel almirah. At that time however, Kaushik, the joint director’s personal assistant came in. So, Meena just slipped the pen drive into the drawer of the table. After Kaushik had gone, he opened the drawer and took out the pen drive to put it into the almirah, but at that moment, the phone had rung. It was his driver, ready to take him home. Then he picked up his bag and left, forgetting about the pen drive.

He called up Dev since he always rose to the occasion and made sure every item in the office was thoroughly checked. Dev said he had not come across any pen drive. Yes, everything had been cleaned and locked up, but nothing had been found. "But don't worry, sir. A very reliable boy, Kishan, is on duty on the third floor," said Dev.

That is what got Meena most worried. Yesterday, Kaushik had come into the room with some pornographic movies on his pen drive. He insisted on showing him one and just as they were engrossed in it, this new boy Kishan stood with a stupid smile on his face, saying someone had come to meet Kaushik. Kaushik told the fellow to go away and they quickly removed the pen drive, then went out. Though Kishan had stood only at the doorway, something about that boy's expression made Meena feel he had caught a glimpse of the screen. Or maybe it was his guilt that made Meena think so. Already Meena was feeling ashamed to be so caught by a security officer was demeaning. The whole night Kishan's face kept coming to Meena in his dreams.

By eight in the morning, Meena was in office. Dev was waiting for him. "He is such an institution," thought Meena as they unlocked the doors and went inside. Of course, they did not find the pen drive. Every person who came in was subject to very close scrutiny and finally—they found it in Kishan's lunch box.

"Why did you not tell me? Even at night you could have told me. Kishan *beta*, why, why, why?" asked Dev several times, his anguish filling the air.

When Dev visited Kishan in prison for the last time, Kishan had become half his size. Everyone in the office believed he was not a spy. Everyone listened to him when he told them why he took the pen drive and what he did with it. Everyone believed him. Everyone.

But why could no one do anything to save that young boy who had his whole life ahead of him? Why did he have to spend it all in prison?

The director had to ask for the documents again. The Defence Ministry asked for reasons and Kishan's remiss action had been brought to their notice. He was arrested under the Official Secrets Act. Dev knew no one who had been arrested under this Act had ever come out of jail. They normally died there. There could be no conclusive proof that he did not pass the information to anyone—a small act of violence would then be ascribed to this leak. The files were also TOP SECRET, the ones he had deleted. Who could say he had not given the information to anybody? Kishan's word did not count. But Kishan was so young…Dev's heart cried. That Kishan had been jobless for three years, that he had viewed the pen drive on a stolen laptop, were not facts that went in his favour.

Knowing all this, Dev still felt it was his duty to plead for the boy, at least for the sake of his friend's wife, who was grief-stricken. He was the only one who pleaded every now and then, even after he retired. He pleaded for mercy, he pleaded for compassion, he pleaded for a life. He just kept pleading…

The Appointed Hour

I had been waiting for her for the past half hour. Actually, I had woken up thinking of this meeting…so in a sense I was waiting since then. We were meeting for lunch. When I reached the restaurant, I attempted to relax by beginning with a drink myself, maybe a starter, maybe browse through a book…all aimed at distracting myself. I gave in to a steadily rising anger as 29 minutes passed. The waiter had come to me twice asking if I was ready to place an order. Did I detect that faint sympathetic smile saying, "Oh so sorry your guest for lunch is not showing up."

Now she better have a good reason I thought. And then I saw her entering. She looked as charming as usual and her body language was indicative of her hurry.

If she said, "I was caught in traffic, it was just impossible!" I would know she was just bluffing. Traffic is the oft-used word used for one's own sloth. You have maps which advise you on how to plan your travel so as to reach on time, with all directions laid out along the route of least traffic by the GPS and so if there was traffic, she should have taken that into consideration and left half an hour earlier. Then I would know what kind of person she was...lazy, gives excuses easily, not professional.

Or perhaps she would say, "You know there was a dreadful accident on our way." Or that, "There was VIP movement and roads were blocked." I would then say she is resourceful, but still lazy.

She was wearing a pink sari with a mauve border. As I watched her, I thought if she was to say, "I was on a conference call which just would not end," or if she said, "My last meeting just went on and on," she wanted to tell me she was a busy person and had back-to-back meetings. I could predict that she would plonk herself on the chair and say something like, "Ah, at last some time...I am so hungry!" Then I would know she was insecure and was trying to impress me. She was still unprofessional and lazy. I would know how to deal with her.

Her brown leather tote seemed full as she swung it on her right shoulder and meandered between tables to reach me. Such a big and heavy bag...maybe she had clutter all around her too. Maybe her coming late is also evidence of her being disorganised. However, if she told me, "I had to pick up my daughter from the bus stop before coming here and the bus was late," I would soften a little towards her but would tell her that she should have scheduled our meeting time half an hour later. Maybe I would teach her something about how to manage children and work. I would give her a second chance.

Her thick and luscious hair was tied back in a bun. Rather conventional, I thought, considering most people had short hair these days. Her face was radiant, as if she was just emerging from a beauty parlour. Aha! Maybe that is why she is late, I chuckled to myself. She did look well turned out. If she told me with a sigh and shrug of her shoulders that she found it, "…so difficult to be on time," I would decide she was best for dinner parties, not to work with. It reminded me of the lame excuses people used to make in those days. There were times when people would say, "Oh! My watch stopped!" I am not joking, but that used to be a good excuse in the good old days when not everyone wore a watch that worked all the time—among other reasons for it to stop working was that the watch had to be wound every day, and often one forgot. If one forgot to wind the watch, it would naturally stop working and you would have to ask a passerby what the time was. Today with mobiles, one does not remember those days. Another age-old excuse worth mentioning, was, "I tried calling you but you must have left by then, your phone kept ringing," or "My phone was dead so I could not call you to say I would be late." Without mobile phones, one was dependent on landlines. A heavy shower, an electricity failure, repair work being carried out somewhere far away…anything could leave the landline dead. And even if not dead, landlines were not always in best condition.

She smiled as she caught sight of me, a warm smile. I observed that the shade of her lipstick matched her sari perfectly. I was more convinced the beauty parlour was the reason for the delay. Or perhaps she could say, "My aged mother had to be given her medicines." That would be a reason for delay that I would have to accept and again, give her another chance.

The reason given is important. I remember when I was about 10 or 11 years of age and was marched into my principal's office for being late to school, I just stood silent. I was late. I could have given many reasons. The bus broke down. My cat was missing. Had to help my mom get breakfast to the table. Dad had an accident. Grandmother died. There were so many possibilities that I could think of, but I kept quiet because I was not so clever those days. "And what is the explanation?" boomed my principal. It was then that I realised an explanation, a reason was required for everything. And the reasons are not always easy to articulate. As a young boy, I could not tell my principal the real reason, which was that my brother took longer in the bathroom. I learnt to lie. I learnt to give plausible, believable reasons…I found that made the person listening to me in control of the situation. Made them feel they "understood". Not necessarily because one believes the reason given, but because one slots or categorises or boxes that person as being such and such and so develops one's strategy of how to strike a relationship with them.

It was such an enticing discovery that I decided to make it my profession and started earning my living by it. I became a novelist. But that had no bearing on why I was waiting for the reason this lady would give me for being late. I was peeved to have been made to wait. My ego was hurt. And so, as her perfume came close to me, I started breathing a little heavily. Should I let my pique show? Am I taking her too seriously? It would all depend on what she said. What would she say? And she said in a friendly tone, "You are early! I thought I would get here before you!"

I made some sounds which I cannot spell out for I then realised I had indeed got here half an hour earlier than our scheduled time of meeting.

ACKNOWLEDGEMENTS

A Collective Effort

To write acknowledgments is always a challenge. Many influences, many people, many experiences build into an idea. To identify each and acknowledge them is impossible. My overarching sense of gratitude defies expression.

My gratitude to K.P.R. Nair for seeing merit in the manuscript. I am thankful to my editor Priyanka Misra for her patience, support and understanding.

I fondly recollect my conversations with my friend Gita Abraham. She was in Canada and I was in the US. She would read and edit my stories and we would have long telephonic discussions on them. Thank you, Gita.

The stories were written at different points of time. One of them titled "Roses are Forever" was first published in a magazine called *Leisure and Treasure* in the February of 1986. The magazine wound up soon after (not because they published my story!)

One day, my dear friend and writer Humra Quraishi and I were talking about the manuscripts that still lay in our computers, unpublished. It was her insistence and persistence that made me compile the stories and pursue their publication. I owe this effort to her. One more candle lit to her memory.

I am thankful to Shriti Nath, editor of different publications and my long-time friend, who goes to bed late and wakes up early, primarily because on most days her WhatsApp pings with a note from me saying, "Please read…." And she does.

In another corner of India, this friend could be travelling or writing to meet deadlines, but when she sees my message, "Aruna, are you free?", she would know it was a call for help. Aruna Srinivasan, bilingual author and dear friend for aeons, would respond immediately and with a comforting answer. My gratitude to her.

My father and mother played pivotal roles in my learning to enjoy words, language and literature. The stories "A Heaven Out of Reach", "Custom-Made" and "Josiyar Ayya" have major inputs from my mother. Can I thank her just for them?

To the rest of my precious family, I am always grateful.

About the Author

Sudhamahi Regunathan served as the vice chancellor of Jain Vishva Bharati Institute (Deemed University) in Ladnun, Rajasthan. She has since contributed to higher education in different capacities.

A prolific author, she has several books across different religious beliefs to her credit, including *Siku: Faith and Conversion*: *Donyipolo Movement in Arunachal Pradesh*, *The Colours of Desire on the Canvas of Restraint*: *The Jaina Way*, *Taken Away: The Ordinary Life of a Lama* and *The Immortal King: Yama*, among others.

She has translated more than a dozen books in both prose and verse, among which *Anekanta: The Third Eye*, *Anekanta in the Context of Jainism*, *The Sound of Silence*, *Rishabhayan: The Story of the First King* and *Vasudeva: The Wanderer Prince* are a few.

She also writes for children with *Folk Tales from the North-East*, *Hanuman: The Flying Hero*, *Ramayana for Babies* and *Ganesha for Babies* being some of the titles.